Saints Row

Book 1

Elizabeth Blair

VPK PUBLISHING
LITTLE ROCK ◇ DALLAS

Saint's Row: Book One /Elizabeth Blair -- 1st ed.
ISBN 13: 978-0-9982371-0-7
ISBN 10: 0-9982371-0-8

He that falleth into sin is a man
That grieves at it, a saint
That boasteth of it, a devil

—THOMAS FULLER

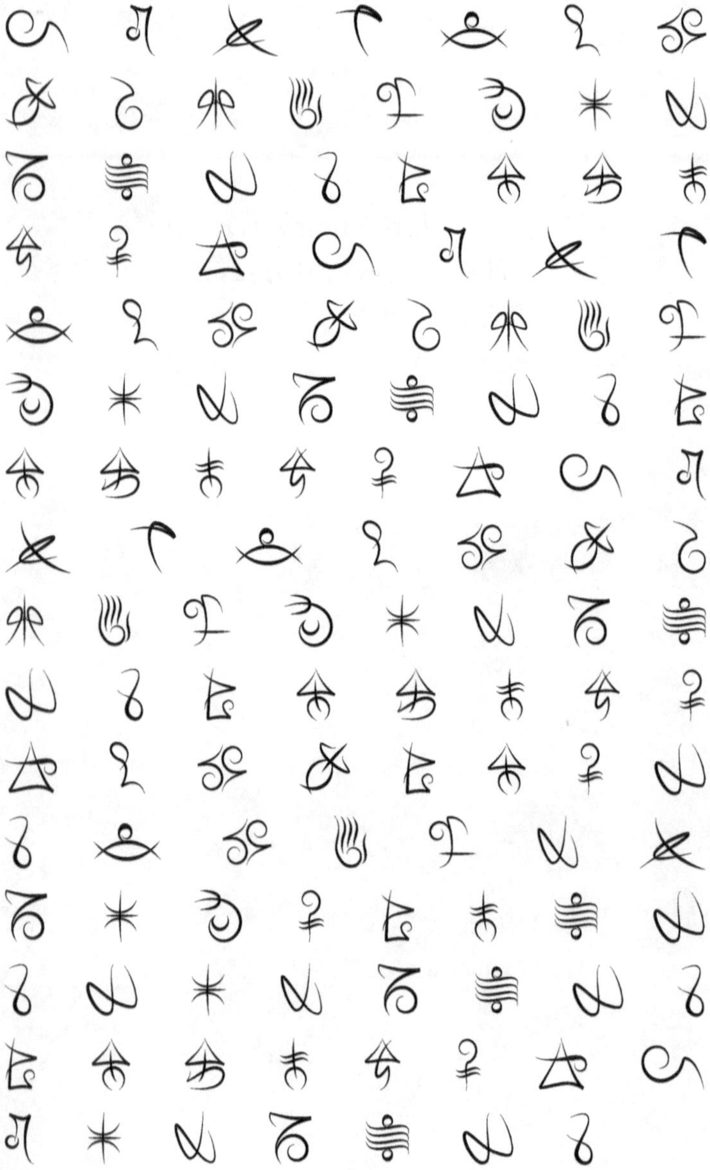

CHAPTER ONE

Cael

From my perch in the shadows of the club, my target was easy to identify. I had been watching him for almost an hour, analyzing his every sideways glance, each ragged breath that could indicate he was ready to strike. But there was nothing, and I could almost believe I'd been given this assignment out of pure spite for my recent misbehavior. The guy seemed harmless: a loner, a bad dresser, piss poor taste in alcohol and enrobed with the stench of a man that still lived in his parent's basement playing video games. Awkward and pathetic, yes, but a serial rapist that plagued the city night after night for weeks on end? I wasn't quite convinced. I tasted the air for some hint of desperation, of unbridled lust, or even murderous tendencies but sensed nothing. Well, nothing related to him anyway.

A few minutes after taking up my post, I was assaulted by a dozen different emotions emanating from one girl. Woman. She was definitely a woman. Although emotions could flicker, usually a person was pretty consistent: if angry, they are angry for a while; if horny, they stay that way until either satisfied or another emotion takes over; if happy, it's in play until something breaks in to dissolve it. Not her. She'd walked in with her own bottle of tequila, never once approaching the bar, and every shot she swallowed sent a myriad of mixed emotions into the atmosphere. It didn't help my distraction that she was so damn easy on the eyes.

Her hair was almost as dark as my own but livened with streaks of red and copper. Natural, from the sun, if the freckles along her shoulders were any indication. Average height, I guessed, but since she'd kicked off her shoes before hitting the dance floor, I couldn't tell. Nor did I really give a damn. It was the curve of her thighs, the dip at her waist, and the long lines of her arms as they flowed into her neck that was making me dizzy. I'd been back for less than twenty-four hours and, if I was going to be here, I might as well celebrate with a wild ride in bed. After watching her curl around a handful of men just to discard them when the song ended, I knew she'd more than qualify.

Most tourists come to New Orleans to get drunk, laid or high, so I had few reservations about making a move on her. Yet there was something, aside from the fact that I was technically working, giving me pause. Something off that I couldn't quite place. Maybe it was just because she was so damn drunk she had a million different emotions coursing through her and I couldn't delineate any of them.

"Still no move?"

My gaze flickered to see my brother, *my boss*, hovering over me. "Ethan, please tell me you did not come to babysit me on my first night back?"

He pushed a double shot of bourbon my direction. "I came to buy you a drink. So no move yet?"

"No, nothing. Are you sure he's the one?"

"Are we ever wrong?"

No. The Saints were never wrong. If they'd determined he was the one responsible for raping a dozen girls in the span of less than a month, then I had no reason to doubt. I was just petulant after being handed this assignment within minutes of arriving back in town and now getting a damned chaperone. It felt like punishment. It *was* punishment. Even so, the target would be handled. I just had to wait him out.

I relaxed back into my chair, sipping the drink, and allowing my eyes to drift back to the girl. What was it about her? Gorgeous and sexy, yes, but she seemed almost invisible to everyone else in the room. How was that even fucking possible? Before I could cut off my curiosity, Ethan had sensed it and was turning her direction.

"Is she drunk or did someone slip her something?"

"She was drunk when she waltzed in, and she's had seven shots of tequila in the last," I glanced down at my watch, "thirty-nine minutes. She's long past the drunk stage, and more at the 'can't remember her own name' phase."

Ethan straightened, his fists digging deep into his pockets. His eyes were locked on her as she twirled the dance floor and I knew he was checking my observation, grading me to see if I was right. I expected to sense curiosity of his own but, instead, was greeted with worry...and recognition.

"Wait, you know her?"

"Yes," he mumbled, "and look somewhere else for the night. There are much easier ways to get laid in the Quarter than that one."

He was telling me she was off limits...at least for now. Irrational emotions bubbled inside me: defensive, protective, jealous. How absurd. I'd never even seen her before tonight. "So who is *that one*?"

"Becca Riley. Her mother died unexpectedly, and she and her sister were the sole beneficiaries. Becca got the house a few blocks from here and her sister, Sarah, got a store down on Jackson Square. Their father was never in the picture. Both single, never married."

"You seem to know a hell of a lot about her. Sounds almost like you're reading a dossier."

"Yes," he admitted, frowning. "She has a nasty habit of being around whenever we have an assignment. Due diligence and all, we did some digging. There's a pretty thick file on her back at the Row."

The Row. Home. The place I'd run from, escaped from, a year ago in hopes of burying the dark visions that were tearing apart my soul. Only to find the farther I ran, the blacker and more violent they became. I took a swallow of bourbon to steady myself, my eyes riveting back toward *that one*.

"And it has nothing to do with how fucking hot she is?"

She was pulling her hair up in a haphazard bun on top of her head, drips of sweat glistening down on the back of her neck and rolling down her spine. She bent down to slip her shoes back on, giving us a clear view straight down her tank top: firm, round breasts hidden behind white lace. Not overly large but thankfully real, full, and so fucking inviting. I could almost taste every bit of her from across the room: salty sweat, sweet lime, and fiery tequila. A low groan rose from my throat without warning as I fought to tear my gaze away and Ethan chuckled.

"Well, I didn't say anyone *complained* about following her around."

"She a journalist? News reporter? Thrill junkie?"

"No, a photographer. If you've seen a photo from the refugee camps in Sicily in the news lately, ones that made you want to vomit and adopt each kid at the same time, pretty sure you were looking at her work."

Praise did not come easily to Ethan and that made my eyes travel her way again. If she could get him to feel anything, then she had to be talented.

"It's always dark, gritty types of things. She seeks it out, and her curiosity tends to make her cross paths with us quite frequently. Also gets her damn close to getting killed on a regular basis. So, like I said, much easier lays can be had."

"If I wanted easy, I wouldn't have come back."

"She's not a damsel in distress, Cael. Trouble always seems to find her, but she's not looking for a savior."

"Saving her is not what I had in mind."

"You might want to reconsider because your target? He just found his target." He nodded toward the man I'd been shadowing. "I told you, she and danger are a magnetic force."

I had discounted the man earlier, but now there was something different, something intense, that etched through his every muscle. We couldn't read minds, couldn't see the future or anything helpful like that, but we could discern emotions - taste them, smell them, inhale them as if they were a solid presence. I had been so distracted wanting her myself that I hadn't noticed the atmosphere change. Now that Ethan pointed it out, it was inescapable: my scumbag serial rapist wanted *that one* with such maddening desperation it was almost suffocating. Ethan even gagged a little as the emotion grew too thick when he sauntered past us.

"Introduce me."

"Cael-"

"Now," I commanded, gripping his arm and shoving him toward the exit.

"Becca!"

She pivoted fast, nearly colliding with her soon to be assailant. She apologized. She fucking apologized as he sidestepped and moved out the door as if he hadn't been aiming for her. When she realized who had called her name, her eyes narrowed.

"Ethan, are you stalking me again or is this just co-incidence?"

My eyes flashed his direction. We were supposed to be ghosts, blending in and going unnoticed was the most basic tenet of our job. She'd known he put her under scrutiny which explained both his caution and her irritation.

"Coincidence, I swear. My brother is back in town, and we're celebrating."

"Another Saint brother?" she breathed. "How fucking many of you are there? Sorry, no offense."

"I wonder that on a regular basis myself." I could see her trying to survey me, but the alcohol was fogging her every move. I offered my hand, but she was so wobbly she couldn't accept it on the first try. "Cael Saint and you are Becca Riley."

"Of course I am. Ethan's probably told you my life story and my bra size by now."

Ethan blushed. He actually blushed, and I could taste his embarrassment in the air. God save us all.

"30C."

"Now that's cleared up, I'm on my way out-"

"Where?" I asked, stalling, hoping to give the scum-bag time to find a different obsession. I didn't believe he would be that easily dissuaded but I had to try.

"Pardon?"

"Where are you headed?"

Her eyes narrowed on me this time, but it was Ethan she whirled on. My arm flashed out to steady her before she could fall. She nodded her thanks but was still intent on him. "I thought we were done with this. I've stayed out of the Tremé for the last two weeks. I turned down the job in Rio based on your intuition, and you promised, you fucking swore, if I did that you would stop with this stalking shit."

No one talks to Ethan like that. He was the eldest, our leader, our patriarch despite his young age. But he was allowing it. Not just allowing but I could sense it all over him: he agreed with her. He had broken their agreement and felt guilty for it. I hesitated, rethinking his words and wondering if I'd stumbled into some bizarre form of seduction between them.

"I'm not stalking you, Becca, but I can see how you might think-"

"Ethan, I've had way too much tequila to deal with you tonight." She exhaled and nodded to me. "I won't say nice to meet you but, welcome back, Cael."

I smiled but was whirling on Ethan before she stalked away. "What the fuck?"

"I warned you."

"You warned me trouble follows her around. You failed to mention you've had the family tailing her, that she's observant enough to pick up on it, or that you've resorted to making deals with her. Did you not think any of that relevant?"

"If you'd been here, you would have known."

"What are you, twelve? You want to pay me back for leaving when a woman's life is at stake? Seriously?"

"Fuck," he growled. His chastising had made him forget the whole reason for our presence. Before I could take a breath, he was lunging out the door. A string of more curse words came out as he tried to pinpoint the direction they'd gone.

I put a hand on his shoulder, calming him. I waited a few seconds as our senses began to intermingle, our abilities much stronger when we acted together. Desperation and need washed over us in a long wave but that was normal for this area...there were too many drunk college kids lusting around to be able to use that as an indicator. I tried to search out fear but found nothing.

"Defiance," Ethan mumbled. "She'll be defiant, not afraid."

Sure enough, the moment the word filtered into my mind, I could feel it like lightning shocking through my every nerve. They were close. He hadn't allowed her to get far.

"I'll take him. You take her."

"He's my assignment-"

"Consider it my apology for acting like a fucking child."

I nodded, and we separated, each taking a different route to the same destination. There was no tension, no surges of adrenaline. Protecting people was the only reason we existed, the only reason we were created. For us, it was as compulsive as breathing. I turned the corner into the alley first and, seeing her fighting against the scum, I knew this was why Ethan had been so cautious about her: it was innate in us to protect, and the last thing *that one* wanted was to be shielded from anything. Unfortunately for her, I am not nearly as accommodating as Ethan where humans are concerned.

*⚘🎶

Becca

Getting groped in a New Orleans alley is a regular thing. Hell, full blown alley sex is a thing here, and I can't say I've never imbibed. But what the hell gave this creeper the idea he would get lucky? Over on Bourbon, he could probably find several willing girls for a handful of bills but, instead, he's got his hands pawing me. I shove him away with the most grace I can manage and mumble a "sorry, not tonight, buddy" before trying to slip away. He's insistent. This time, he is back on me, harder and more punishing. It takes several minutes for the tequila haze to lift, and I actually realize my situation: he isn't trying to get lucky but trying to force me.

A vague memory of news reports on a serial rapist a few weeks earlier comes to mind, but everyone assumed he was a tourist and had moved on. Now I knew better...he'd either been waiting for the news to die down or had just been more discreet. Lucky me, he's now over that. I thrust him into the wall, impatience rushing through me. I am too drunk and too furious to deal with this tonight. For chrissakes, I'm only a few blocks from home! Before I could strike at him again, Ethan Saint's face swam into view and the man was wrenched away.

I teetered, but strong arms had me caged against the brick in seconds. His body crushed into mine like stone. No, not like stone. I'd been with strong men before - men hardened from working out, muscles chiseled from hours in the gym. But this was different. It *was* stone. Hard, brittle, unmoving even when breathing, and completely inescapable. Before I was angry but now? Now I was fucking terrified.

"Him you want to fight, but you're afraid of me?" he laughed. "Your judgment needs some work, sweetheart."

His voice dripped with warmth and invitation. It wrapped me in a cocoon of comfort and protection that totally did not make sense considering the dominating position he had locked me in. I could hear the fight behind him - the screams, the cursing, the pain, and agony. But I could see nothing but Cael's dark t-shirt. Yes! His name was Cael. I remembered!

"Your emotions are so fucking errant," he grumbled. "Are you always like this or is it the tequila?"

"Tequila." I dropped my head onto his chest as my head continued to spin, not caring if I didn't know him. I *did* know Ethan. Well, I knew he was determined to keep me from getting hurt, so I assumed that extended to his brother. Not his brother. They couldn't actually be related. Even drunk I wasn't that stupid, but their family tree wasn't any of my business.

I exhaled as I tried to get my brain to quiet. My breath against his body caused his shirt to flutter, and a wave of scent bounced back at me: rain, earth, sunshine. How could you smell like sunshine? My whole body tensed with confusion which made him tense in return.

"What's the matter?" I didn't answer, and he pressed closer, his voice soothing. "It'll be over soon, and we'll see you home."

"He's killing him?"

"Yes." He inhaled, almost as if he was checking the air. "You're surprised."

"I'm surprised you admitted it."

"Right now I'd admit almost anything to you."

His words gave me temporary clarity, and I became aware of how each hard muscle was pushing into my softer frame. I would have bruises tomorrow from the bricks biting into my back, from his granite touch but tonight I relished them. I could feel his thighs locking my entire body in place, his hips hard against my ribs and his cock...long, thick and rigid against my waist. I knew better than to think it was the violence that he found enticing. At least I hoped so. Curious, I shifted and raked my breasts against him. His body was so hard, so unyielding, that my nipples pebbled instantly, and I could feel a stirring of tequila-fueled warmth light between my thighs. I shifted again, rubbing myself deeper along him as I tested how well our bodies might fit together.

"I didn't realize how tiny you are," he whispered, resting his chin on my head.

Not the words I wanted to hear from his mouth. I gave a frustrated sigh. "Tiny and needing to be protected, right?"

This time, he was the one who moved. His head dropped lower, his lips hovering just beneath my ear. One of the arms caging me dropped, tracing a slow, seductive line down my side. "Actually, I was thinking how I can probably hold you in one arm when I take you which leaves my other open for so many additional possibilities."

Nearly raped in an alley. Someone being killed paces away. In the arms of a man whose name I could barely remember and the single consuming thought in my head was how much I wanted him to fuck me senseless until every stray thought vanished from my mind. I had no doubt he could do it. If anyone could, it would be him. I could feel his cock twitch against me, and I let out a shuddering breath.

"Interesting," he purred. "Desire is the one emotion you allow no other to invade. No, not interesting. Mesmerizing and erotic as fucking hell. Is that the tequila as well?"

"No."

"No?"

"You seem surprised."

"Surprised you admitted it." He chuckled then glanced over his shoulder. "Ethan, stop playing before I do something really stupid here. We need to get her home."

"Yeah, yeah." A sharp snap, a thud, and then Ethan was beside us. "Can I at least get a thank you this time?"

I had to grit my teeth to say the words. "Thank you."

"That's the tequila talking, isn't it?" he asked, raising an eyebrow.

"Yes."

"Christ, Becca, do you have no sense of self-preservation?" He took my arm, pulling me forward in the direction of my house.

I glanced back, but Cael was already at my other side. Now that I was moving again, the alcohol was back rushing through my system, and I took their arms to keep from stumbling on the bricks. I stopped mid-stride, allowing them to steady me as I tugged off my shoes. I tested my balance, decided it better, and started walking again. "He eats the air like you do."

"What?"

"To try and read people."

I could see their eyes lock over my head, and I laughed. "I don't have to eat the air, just for the record. For example, right now Cael is trying to figure out exactly what you and I have going on. Hoping to hell he wasn't just making salacious suggestions to a woman *his brother* has already laid claim to, and Ethan is furious that I can't seem to stay out of trouble. Like I'm his own personal demon sent from hell to test his resolve."

"You have an active imagination," Ethan grunted.

"I live in New Orleans. Eating air, reading emotions? Not even close to the weirdest fucking things I've come across in this city."

Ethan stopped us this time, his fingers tightening on my biceps. "You aren't the drink until you pass out type. Want to tell us what were you trying to drown tonight, Becca?"

"Touché," I murmured. "You have your secrets, and I have mine."

"That wasn't-"

"Here." I nodded toward the house; where a lantern was still lit waiting for my arrival. Now that I was here, true safety so close, I felt calmer and more assured. More myself. I turned to them both, drinking in their care and concern for a woman that was pretty much a stranger. It was devastatingly sexy, and humiliating after the way I'd treated them.

I stretched up and kissed Ethan on the cheek. "Thank you. Really. That could have gone so horribly bad. And you," I turned to Cael, and I knew he could sense the amusement I was feeling. "Ethan thinks of me as a little sister. If I even say the word cock, the man flushes with embarrassment. So that suggestion of yours? Consider me game to try."

"Tequila?" Cael questioned.

I grinned. "Guess you'll have to catch me sober to find out."

"That," Ethan sighed, "is more the Becca I know. Challenging little shit."

"Give my best to your army of brothers."

"Give my regards to that sexy sister of yours."

"Thankfully," I grumbled, "she doesn't even know you exist."

Ethan laughed. "That can be remedied. Night, Becca."

CHAPTER TWO

Becca

"God, you look awful."

"So gracious, Sarah" I mumbled, tugging a pillow back over my head to block out the light. I fought against her as she pulled it away but I still wasn't coherent enough to win. "Tell me you have coffee."

"Double strength," she said and waved the mug in front of me. "What happened to you last night?"

"You wouldn't believe me."

She pushed my legs aside and sank onto the bed, taking a drink of my coffee. I sat up slow, dragging a hand through my knotted mess of hair.

"I'd believe anything in this town. Vampires convert you? Ghosts track you home? Cats steal your breath? Or something more devilish like an asshole slipping something into your drink?"

The night washed over me in full force, and I curled back down, resting my head in her lap. "All of the above if the amount of tequila I consumed is any indication."

Her hand went to my head, stroking it and my eyes drifted closed under the soft, rhythmic pattern. "Do you want to tell me?"

I shook my head and just let her comfort me. Ethan had been right: I wasn't the drink until you drop type. I wasn't even the emotionally unstable girl that I was exhibiting this morning. But yesterday had been a bad day or, at least an anniversary of a very bad day. Usually, I could handle anything, but some switch had flipped last night, and I just didn't a shit about holding myself together anymore.

"It was the anniversary, wasn't it?" she asked, whisper soft. "Of the attack on mom."

I nodded but refused to let the tears fall in her presence.

"Why didn't you say something? You know I would've-"

"I know." I sat up, offering the best smile I could fake, and snagged the mug away. "I'm fine. I just needed to get drunk and forget for a little while. Besides, you had a hot date and who am I to interfere when my sister finally has a remote chance of getting laid?"

"Becca-"

"Please, let's not go there, okay?"

"You sure?"

"Positive."

She ruffled my hair like I was a ten-year-old but grinned at me. "Then let me grab my coffee, and you can catch me up on what went right last night."

"What do you mean?"

"I'll grab the deliveries and be back right back to show you."

I struggled up, determined to at least get my teeth brushed before she returned. I'd just managed to climb back onto the bed when she returned with a fresh pot and a stack of packages. As she poured the coffee, I thumbed through, but nothing caught my attention. A few letters from my agent, boxes of some prints I had ordered, random junk mail, and a letter from a local gallery that would be exhibiting my photographs next week. I shrugged, tossed them all aside, and gave her an expectant glance. "Still not following, sis."

She gave me an exasperated hiss and pulled a squarish, cream colored envelope from the pile. I flipped it over, noting the old fashioned red wax seal. Sarah was bouncing on the mattress, almost like a kid at Christmas. It was making me nauseous, and I tossed the envelope back before running to the restroom. I dry heaved a few times before remembering I hadn't eaten last night. She draped a cold cloth on the back of my neck but the envelope was still twitching in her opposite hand.

"You don't know what this is, do you?" she prompted, leading me back to the bed. "It's stationary. From the Saint Foundation."

I gazed at her blankly even though my chest began to tighten.

"The Saint Foundation? Saint's Row?" Her voice was rising, and she shook it at me. "The most exclusive place in the entire city? Where presidents and princes go? Seriously, Becca?"

"I've heard of it."

Of course, I had. It was an estate in the Garden District that was known to have better security than the White House. Their annual parties and occasional fundraisers drew international attention but, locally, they were known for their darker side. Wild parties, disappearances, an atmosphere where anything and everything was not only accepted but expected.

"How do you know any of them and how could you not introduce me?"

"I don't know-" I trailed off. No. They wore jeans and t-shirts. They drank bourbon and beer and roamed the streets at all hours. They murdered people. For a good cause but still...they ate the air, for chrissakes! My Saint brothers could not be *the* Saints. I'd been crossing paths with Ethan for months now and surely there would have been some giveaway that he was part of a philanthropic, global political force. It just couldn't be the same people. It was a common name here, wasn't it? I'd thought it like Jones or

Smith. I exhaled and took the envelope from her. There were only a few words, written in old-fashioned calligraphy. "It's an invitation to a party on the *Crescent Queen.*"

"The steamboat being refurbished? Oh my god, Becca! Do you know the celebrities that have backed that deal?" She was bouncing again, and I was afraid she might squeal in her glee. "There's something else on the back."

I flipped it over, and the elegant scrawl turned me inside out. *Stay safe and sober ~ Cael.*

"We're going, right? Tell me we're going!"

"Sarah-"

I was not up to a party. I was not up to socializing of any sort. Last night had been proof enough of that. Smiling, mingling, making banal chatter to strangers? Not the way I wanted to spend my evening. Wine, a cozy robe, and a movie marathon were much more my speed at the moment. I glanced at her and could see the disappointment wash over her. She knew I was going to say no, and it was devastating her. I might not have ever dreamed of attending one of their parties, but clearly, she had. And it would be great networking for the store. Mom's store. How bitchy could I be? I gave a single nod, and she launched herself at me, yanking me into a fierce hug.

"You are the best! I'll take care of everything. Find dresses, shoes, everything. You just sleep, okay?"

She was gone in seconds, and I curled back onto the bed, waiting for sleep to come. When it didn't, I scooped my laptop from the side table and searched up the Saint Foundation. There was the information I already knew: their political connections; photos of a gorgeous estate; selfies from people claiming to be at the wilder of the parties. The Foundation had no website of their own, no listings in the charity databases, and the only photograph that ringed "official" was a group of men at the laying of the cathedral cornerstone in 1789 with the caption "Saint's Row Realized." Whatever the fuck that meant. I shut the computer off in frustration, my head pounding.

I fell back into the down comforter, sorting through the memories of the night before. I could remember all the elements if not the exact details, but there was one thing I could not deny: Cael Saint. Everything about him was undeniable. His mysterious nature, his protective stance, the way his smell overwhelmed my senses, and his voice thrummed dark and warm against my throat. I hadn't even gotten a good look at him, but he was dangerous and safe at the same time which piqued my curiosity and caused my body to ache. He probably made lots of women feel that way, but I didn't care. It wasn't as if I hadn't had one night stands before and this week? This week I was game for anything that could make me forget.

✳✗♯

Cael

I threw my punch hard, taking pleasure in the pain as blood began to drip from my knuckles. In New York, boxing had been about survival. Here, it was purely a stress reliever. I hugged the bag to catch my breath, dropping my head against the scratchy canvas. My eyes landed on the table across the room where a four-inch-thick file kept calling. One of the men had delivered it an hour before but I still couldn't bring myself to open it. Four inches of investigations into Becca Riley's life. A well done and thorough job from the look of it, but an invasion of her privacy that I couldn't bring myself to breach.

"Let me see," Ethan ordered. He tapped my hands, cupping them in his own. "Sit down. I'll rewrap them for you."

I dropped into the metal chair two strides away as he began cutting off the bloodied bandages.

"You're not going to read it are you?" he asked. "I couldn't read Sarah's either, and hers was only like three pages. Maybe we're getting too old for this shit."

"Or maybe we're finally mature enough to separate personal from professional."

"Unfortunately, your girl is both."

Not what I wanted to hear. I dropped my head back, closing my eyes. A splash of alcohol burned into my flesh before I felt the fresh tape wind tight around my palms. He rapped them hard. "Good to go."

I began pummeling the bag once more, but he was following close behind. He leaned into the opposite side, steadying the bag while scowling at me.

"Fine," I grumbled. "Fine. Just tell me."

He told me the facts, cold and hard like reading a script. She'd shown up at several assignments, the wrong place at the wrong time kind of thing. Never intentional but she just always seemed to have some bad element in her midst. Which wasn't surprising...her own assignments or predilections or whatever, led her into wars, refugee camps, gang fights and human trafficking rings.

"A tiny fireball not afraid to go anywhere."

"Then what was that last night?" I asked, stopping to catch my breath. "She wasn't drowning out a bad week, Ethan. I may be a little out of practice, and the tequila had her mind in chaos, but even I couldn't miss the blind fucking terror hidden in there."

I raised my arm for another punch but pulled it back mid-throw. Ethan's face was pale; his eyes furrowed together. I tried to search out, to determine his mood.

"Won't work," he murmured. He waved his hand upward, circling the room. My eyes followed, noting the narrow band of etched wood that trimmed the wall where it met the ceiling. "I had the runes etched while you were gone. This was always your favorite room. Now it can be a sanctuary as well."

The runes are our one source of protection against emotions. I leave the study of them to the scholars, but I do know they are as ancient as the founding of the first churches. Since emotions can be both light and dark, the runes were also a balance of both. When placed, they act as an invisible shield to block out emotions. Each of our bedrooms was etched to give us sanctuary from even the other Saints - the one place we could experience true quiet and tranquility. The public areas of the Row were left unmarked so that we could still discern the emotions of our many visitors. Ethan taking notice of my love for the gym and going to the trouble of having it etched was one of the reasons he was such a damn good leader. But it still didn't get him off the hook.

"Thoughtful, but it just means we'll have to do this the old-fashioned way." I stepped to the bag, closing in on him. "Tell me about you and Becca Riley."

He opened his mouth, then closed it. A ripple of unease traveled up my spine, and my voice became more urgent. "Ethan."

"Let's get out of here," he managed. Without waiting for an answer, he strode to the door and tossed me my discarded shirt. Ethan is the calm one, the one never phased by anything. It's why he's our patriarch. All of that calm demeanor had vanished, and even without my extra abilities, I knew he was completely off kilter. As I rushed behind him to keep up, the only thought in my head was: if he tells me he loves her, I might just have to fucking kill him.

When we reached the perimeter of the Row, and the runes lost their hold, I skidded to a stop. Anxiety, distress, agitation, and the briefest quiver of melancholy before Ethan could block it away.

He knew I could sense it but said nothing and, instead, flagged down the St. Charles trolley as it rolled close. When the door folded open, he waved a few hundreds at the driver. "Put it out of service."

"You got it, Mr. Saint."

It took a few minutes for the driver to get it emptied out, angering the tourists with his excuses of maintenance issues. When they were all cleared, we hopped on board and took seats opposite each other in the back.

"Where to?"

"Doesn't matter," he answered, not bothering to glance the driver's way. The moment we clattered down the track, Ethan dropped his elbows to his knees and glared at me. "Don't make me regret trusting you, Cael."

I nodded because, well, what the hell else was I supposed to do? I shifted back against the wall of the trolley, angling a leg onto the seat to let him know I was prepared to listen for however long he needed.

"I knew of Sarah and Becca," he paused, "before."

Before. *Before the Saints.* It was the most fundamental of all rules. We were allowed no connection to our life before. We weren't even allowed to live in the same city much less stay in touch with anyone.

"It wasn't long after I joined. I was at the Vatican for additional training-"

"That's a thing?"

"There were," he seemed to be searching for the right word, "*concerns* over my ability to be redeemed. Not the point of this conversation. Read my file if you're that fucking curious."

"I am never letting you live that down, brother," I chuckled.

"Sarah and Becca were there on vacation, I guess. Even then they were impossible to miss. Becca got in trouble for taking photos in a restricted area, and Sarah came to her defense. The Swiss Guard got involved. It was a mess. A crazy, ludicrous mess but still a mess. It's a non-issue. I didn't meet them, talk to them, interact with them in any way, but still-"

He didn't need to say it. He feels obligated, just as any of us would. Any connection to our past was one to be protected, savored, relished...the same reason it was forbidden.

"Cael, no one-"

"Can know," I finished. "I get it."

He would be gone, banished, without a second thought. It wouldn't matter how talented he was, how loyal, how vital to the Row. There was no forgiveness, no second chances in our world. When you live by so few rules, there wasn't much wiggle room.

He'd protected me when I ran. He never reported me, never hinted that my commitment had faltered...he saved me when I couldn't save myself. Now, it was my turn to do the same.

Sarah *was* a non-issue. A local shop owner that he had the hots for, nothing more. Becca was an entirely different story. Her presence at repeated Saint assignments would draw attention eventually, and the thick investigation file would shatter any excuses we might offer. But...there was another option.

As a one-night stand, a regular lover, or even just a friends with benefits arrangement, she would fall under the protective gaze of all the Saints worldwide. Watching out for each other, watching over those we care about - it was expected and encouraged. It would explain why she'd been put under guard, why there was a hefty file on her, and even why she might appear at our assignments. So, technically, all I had to do was bed her. Considering that was already my plan, I wouldn't be sacrificing much.

"I'll handle it."

"Cael, she's not like others."

"I didn't say she was."

"I know you," he argued. "You think you can fuck her, bring her in the fold long enough to protect me, and then toss her. I'm telling you: she will not be so easily discarded."

I chuckled to cover the tension his words invoked in me. "She doesn't seem like the stalker type, Ethan."

"She's not the one I'm worried about."

"Fiery as she may be, I can handle a tiny thing like Becca Riley."

I thought it was the truth, but my senses alerted us both without warning: doubt, suspicion, ambivalence. I was lying, and now we both knew it. Being unable to lie, even to yourself? Yeah, that's a bitch.

CHAPTER THREE

Becca

The *Crescent Queen* was glittering at its moorings, a jewel beckoning to the city's elite. Soft jazz echoed onto the dock and, as decadent as it appeared, I couldn't help but hesitate. I fidgeted with the backless dress Sarah had gotten me, hoping to hell that the draped fabric wouldn't slip any lower. I tugged down the mid-thigh hem and then realized I was just making it worse.

"How the hell do people wear shit like this?"

"If we play our cards right, neither one of us will be wearing them for long," she laughed and tucked her arm through mine to get me moving again. "Stop stressing. No one will ever guess we don't belong here."

"I'm not worried about that."

And I wasn't. Not really. I'd been to embassy parties in dozens of different countries. Granted, I usually had more clothes on, but I'd still managed to mingle as required. I *was* worried about the starry-eyed gleam in Sarah's eyes. I might see Cael as a hot rush of carnal need, but her inclinations to the Saints were floating more into fairytale dreams of shining knights wielding impossible promises.

"Becca, I see you and your sister made it." Ethan was at our side the second we crossed the threshold. "Introduce me to your sister?"

I could feel her gaze drift over him, checking out the muscles, the hand-tailored tux, the sexy scruff that I knew was her downfall. She was instantly smitten. Damn her. "Sarah, this is Ethan Saint. He's been quite determined to meet you."

"And you've prevented this why exactly?" she laughed and sent him a sexy wink that made me twitch. It was like watching your parents make out.

"You look stunning, Sarah. Welcome to the *Queen*." He kissed her hand and then turned a darker look my direction. "You, however...you I feel the need to grab my coat and throw it over your shoulders."

"See?" I hissed.

Sarah's arm draped around me, her eyes narrowing. "My sister looks ravishing."

"I know," he grumbled. "That's the fucking problem."

"If anyone deserves to decompress, it's her. Did you know she got attacked in the alley? Blocks from home."

Ethan's eyes lifted to me, but before either of us could comment, Sarah was talking again.

"I'd drink myself under the table if I was her. Or just stay stoned the entire tourist season."

"Interesting choice," he chuckled and offered her his glass of whiskey. "And you, Becca, is that your plan?"

"I tend not to make plans."

"It will involve men. It always involves men."

"Do you intend to ruin my reputation in one single evening, Sarah?" I gave him an apologetic frown. "She was nervous as hell. She hit our liquor cabinet pretty hard to take the edge off."

"True," Sarah smiled and stepped away to get a re-fill.

"You'll watch out for her?"

"I won't let her leave my side," he promised. "And you-"

"I promise not to make a scene at your fancy-"

"Not one of my concerns. Becca, you catch one Saint, you catch us all. Just remember that, okay?"

"What the hell does that even mean?"

He stepped closer, his hand light on my arm. "It means, we don't share. So don't make a drunken mistake that ruins your chance to get the Saint you really want."

"Did you just call me a whore, Ethan?" I laughed. "The more I get to know you-"

"No, Becca. I know you're hurting. I know you are hiding things from Sarah, and I know that it wasn't just drunk hormones flooding through you when you were in Cael's arms last night. So just don't make a mistake you'll regret."

"Ever my big brother," I grumbled. "Thank you for the concern. Now go take care of my sister before she makes a mistake that *you'll* regret."

His eyes flashed to the bar where Sarah was leaning hard on the shoulder of some stranger, her giggling voice echoing. "Damned Riley women will be the death of all of us," he chuckled then kissed my cheek before setting off to retrieve her.

I turned, slipping a fluted glass off the tray of a passing waiter. Just as I lifted the glass, my eyes found Cael. He was across the room, deep in feigned conversation, and he pursed his lips at me. I sighed and traded the champagne for a bottle of water. I tipped it his direction, and he chuckled. Pride or arrogance...I wasn't sure what emotion he was emanating, but it caused every tuxedo-clad Saint to turn my direction. Territorial. He was laying claim. A shiver of desire mixed with indignation ran up my spine and I exhaled. This was going to be a long fucking night.

I managed to stay around long enough to seem presentable and not undermine Sarah's efforts. She was half toasted, but Ethan's arm was tight around her waist, keeping her in check. He was doting on her, and I had to admit, it was cute. In a nauseating kind of way.

He'd managed to slow her alcohol intake and get some food in her before she could end up like the rest of the revelers. Drunk on free liquor and high on whatever being offered in the private back rooms, the guests would never notice my escape but, no matter how long I waited, there was always a sober Saint in my periphery. When an old grandfather clock chimed one a.m., my last bit of patience evaporated and I made a break for the seclusion of the upper decks. Saint bodyguards be damned.

"You've stayed sober."

I didn't bother to turn but waved my water bottle Cael's direction. "Sadly, yes."

He slipped to the railing and traded my bottle for a champagne flute. "Your anxiety is blaring through our brains like bad zydeco music so, please, have a drink before we all go insane."

I laughed but swallowed the drink. He poured me another, loosening his tie as he watched me finish it as well. "You know this area isn't safe. It's off limits until the refurbishment is completed. There are signs everywhere. Chains even."

"I've always found *off limits* to be a vague term worth investigating."

"You would." He refilled my glass once more before putting the bottle aside and leaning against the railing beside me. "You aren't much for socializing, hm?"

"Not this week. Do I need to worry about Ethan's newfound fascination with my sister?"

"I don't think it's newfound. Her name was on his lips the moment I returned to the city. Do you think you need to worry?"

"Despite the things I don't know, there are several I do. You aren't actually related, you all have an uncanny knack for intervening in the worst trouble in the city, and I have watched at least one of you Saint boys crush a man's larynx with a single hand. So, I repeat, do I need to worry for my sister's safety?

"I take offense to the term *boys*, but no, you do not."

Taking my arm, he slipped it to balance on the railing, his fingers tracing the veins up and down my forearm. I wanted to remain combative, but the move was too silky, too meditative, and I could only manage a soft plea. "Make me believe you."

"We were all chosen for this job for different reasons, but the one thing in common was that we were all pretty useless human beings. We were guilty of being drug dealers, kiddie porn fans, abusers, sexual deviants or a million other lesser crimes. We were the parts of society people wish they could forget. Ethan is the exception. Ethan was in the seminary, on his way to becoming a priest. Illogically, he fell in love. Then she was viciously attacked on the night he intended to propose. His devastation was all consuming and, had the Saints not taken him when they did; he would have destroyed himself and anyone within a ten block radius. For love, Becca. So, no, there is no one on the planet less likely ever to hurt your sister."

I stretched over, kissing the tense muscle along his neck and staying there seconds longer than required so that I could inhale his scent...sunshine in the dead of night. "Thank you."

"Were you afraid your sister is getting involved with a murderer?"

"I *know* she's getting involved with a murderer. It's more the drug dealer, kiddie porn, self-gratification thing that gives me pause."

"You have a very intriguing ethical code."

"I spent time in Syria years ago. I was living with the most amazing family - a father and four of the most precious little girls you've ever seen. When the war reached their home, I watched as he tucked them in bed, read them a bedtime story, and once they were asleep, he slit their throats one by one. When I tried to get him to flee with me, he refused to leave their bedside. They would have been raped, beaten, and sold into slavery where they would have been fucked a hundred times a day, whipped if they ever com-plained, and eventually bludgeoned to death or hanged in public to serve as a lesson for other girls. He saved them from that in the only way he knew how. Technically, he was a murderer four times over. To me, he was a fucking hero."

"That," he whispered, "just told me more about you than reading your emotions ever could."

Well, that was certainly not my intention. I exhaled, trying to let my thoughts settle. His fingers started their soothing trail again, and I smiled. He knew his words had raised my defenses, and he was trying to brush them back down. I tilted my head his direction. "Is it like a sixth sense, then? Your ability?"

"Very accurate way to describe it."

"Can you turn it off?"

"Why?"

"It's unnerving to have you know what I'm thinking."

"I can't read your mind, Becca. It's just your emotions. When strong enough, they rule actions which can make it *seem* like I'm reading your mind but, I promise, I'm not. Like the guy in the alley. He was so consumed with having you; there would be nothing to derail his plans. Other times, emotions are fleeting. Desire that goes unrequited, a fury that tempers itself."

"And did you learn this or inherit it or what?"

"A little of both. Our abilities are bestowed on us by a council of elders, the Concilium Patronis-"

"The Council of Protectors."

"You know your Latin."

"Not hardly, but I do know my Harry Potter."

"Touche," he chuckled. "We learn to use the abilities, train with them, from the other Saints. Leaders like Ethan."

"And-"

"Politicians with ulterior motives and gossip hungry celebrities don't make for the safest party guests."

He squeezed my arm in apology. "I really can't say more right now."

I nodded, accepting. He'd actually given me far more than I expected. I smiled, tipping my glass his direction for a refill. He obliged, but I could see the uncertainty draw across his face.

"You're drowning something again. The party or something else? Not me, I hope."

"Not you," I assured him.

I tilted the flute over the railing, watching the lights glint against the crystal in unsteady rainbows. Champagne, I decided, was useless as a memory quencher. I opened my palm, letting the glass drop three levels down into the gulf. I had to stretch on tiptoes to see it hit the water. When it finally sank, I dropped my heels back down and gave a soft huff. "A year ago my mother was attacked. It was brutal, savage. I was there when it happened. A week later she died from the injuries. So you, the newest Mr. Saint to enter my realm, have caught me at a very, very dark time."

Why did I tell him that? Because I didn't want him to think me a complete drunkard. Because I didn't want him to think I was drowning him. Because I couldn't stand not telling someone. Because he met me on the one week of the entire year that was hell and I didn't want him to take this for the normal me.

He didn't offer a trite "sorry for your loss" or seem to find my admission out of the ordinary. I suppose his ability to read emotions meant he could get just about anyone to admit anything. His body angled toward me, one hand slipping to the bare flesh along my spine. "You regret telling me. That emotion is clear as glass."

I nodded rather than deny it. What was the point? Besides, his touch was sending sparks of electricity down every inch of my skin, and that *was* a memory quencher.

"But the others are much more elusive. Maybe it's because there are so many."

"I am conflicted about many things these days," I admitted. "I imagine I'll be more normal next week if that helps any."

"It would be less intimidating but not nearly as fun," he chuckled. He leaned closer, his breath warm against my ear. "I love a challenge."

"Me too. So let's test you, shall we?"

He frowned. "I'm not sure you want to do that. I'm really very good at my job, and you seem to prefer privacy."

"Coward."

He gave me a lopsided grin. "Amusement and confidence with a flicker of sadness remaining."

I fought down the sadness, trying to bury all thoughts of my mother's death.

"Guilt," he murmured. "And irritation that I'm right. No, irritation at yourself for being predictable. You're not, by the way. This is not at all where I expected this conversation to lead us."

That was all it took for my mind to dissolve into what I really wanted from him. I hadn't stayed sober to have a conversation. I hadn't worn a backless dress sans undergarments in hopes of having a meaningful discussion about our lives. I closed my eyes, letting his close heat wash over me, allowing my body a chance to catch up with my mind. I breathed a long, trembling breath.

"I don't need a sixth sense to know that one." A low growl rose in his throat, and he shuffled behind me, pressing our bodies together. "But what is it you desire, Becca? My touch, my mouth, my-"

If he expected me to be shy or cower at his directness, he was mistaken. I straightened against him, my hands reaching to back to stroke the length of his thighs. "All of you."

His fingers slipped down my back, following the drape of my dress and leaving shivers in their wake. He pushed aside the edges of my dress, wrapping his hands underneath to cup my breasts. His grip tightened harder and then harder still. When I gave no protest, he pinched my nipples, tugging and flicking them in a painful, glorious rhythm. I clasped his hands tighter to me, wanting more.

"You like rough," he murmured. "Why am I not surprised?"

He didn't give me a chance to answer before burying his teeth into the curve of my throat. My body rocked into him, a low desperate moan building. His hand slid lower, over my abdomen and down between my thighs. I was already wet, coating him the moment his hand reached my sex.

"You came with a mission, didn't you, Becca?"

I could barely manage the answer as he made long, slow strokes against my swollen clit. "Yes."

"For me or just anyone?"

Although his fingers were still exploring my folds in teasing circles, something in his voice alerted me to a change. I could feel his cock pressing into me, knew he wanted this as much as I did, but his question was a warning. He would not be used. Was that what I was doing? Maybe.

"Uncertainty," he whispered with a sigh. He didn't rip his hands away as I expected, but his strokes slowed to a stop, and he dragged his hands out of my dress. He held me for a few minutes as my breath calmed, his lips still tracing lines across my back.

"When you want me and not just a quick anonymous screw, come find me. Deal?"

I nodded and turned in his arms, taking a proper look at him for the first time. He stood unmoving, allowing my hands to trail up his arms, fingering each broad indentation of his muscles. I swirled circles against his chest, exploring each ripple on his abdomen before rising on my tiptoes to caress his face. A severe haircut done with almost military precision just like all the other Saints, the same sexy stubble they all wore no matter the time of day, and his eyes...a dark fathomless gray. No, not gray exactly but as if the blue and brown had warred somewhere in his genetics and neither had quite come out the victor. The white wasn't even white but more of a light champagne. I reached my fingers up, brushing around them.

"You've exhausted me," he explained. "Your emotions are devilishly strong."

"Like bleary, red eyes after a crying fit?"

He nodded as his mouth traced against the inside of my arm. "Exactly like that, yes."

"Should I apologize?"

"For your emotions? God, no. For showing up dressed, or undressed, like that? No to that either."

"For anything?" I murmured, and he straightened in my arms.

"Judged? That's a totally new one. I can't say I've ever had that one thrown at me before. Really, Becca, you think I'm judging you?"

The blush rose fast, rising up every inch of my skin.

"Ah, because I said no." He snagged my waist, pulling me tighter against him. "I wouldn't deny anyone the right to a quick shag to banish memories for a little while, but this is my home. It's your home and, if Ethan's right, you and I will be running into each other on a regular basis. If you absolutely have to have that as a release to drown things out then find a tourist. Use them, discard them, whatever. But don't use me. It would be awkward and regrettable for the rest of our days."

Was this his way of brushing me off? That I was too broken and damaged for him to deal with? My emotions too exhausting for him to even bother with? I'm the confident sister! Why the hell was I suddenly feeling rejected like a little school girl?

His hand slipped into mine, sliding it down and pressing it against his cock. Taking my wrist, he slid my palm up and down, allowing me to explore the full length of him. "Becca, for chrissakes," he muttered, "does that feel like rejection? It's a boundary. Nothing more. I'm sure you'll set your own for me in the future as well."

The future. That was promising. That I could accept. He released my wrist, but I kept my hand in place, stroking him in firm, slow beats. Even through his dress pants, he felt like steel in my small hand. Thick, full and shockingly long. I couldn't help the soft purr of appreciation that rose in my throat as I focused on his tip, tracing my fingers around its edge. I wanted him...and I wanted him now. I went to curl my fingers around the width of him, and his hips thrust toward me without warning. A half second later, he had my hand pinned back at his waist.

"I'm a Saint, Becca, not an angel," he groaned. "So I really, really think we need to get you home now."

It took me a few breaths to find my voice. "If you keep sending me home like this I may give up on you and go tourist hopping."

A sexy, crooked grin spread across his face. "I promise, I'm worth the wait."

"Cocky bastard," I laughed and gave him a playful shove that didn't even make him flinch. "Let me off of this boat."

"Bossy suits you. I'll have some of the men escort you home."

"I can-" His eyes narrowed, and I knew that, unlike Ethan, there would be no negotiating. He was not going to allow me to travel home alone. "And Sarah?"

"If I'm not mistaken, she'll be spending the night with Ethan. He's quite smitten."

"The two of them have appointed themselves my guardian angels. I don't think I can handle them working in tandem."

He laughed and put his hand on the small of my back to lead me away. "From what I've learned, you need about a hundred guardians to keep you safe."

If only my mother had some. Even one or two might have kept her safe. I bit my lower lip as the memories surged until I felt a single convulsion rip through Cael's body. I knew my emotions were back swirling, and it had to be killing him. "Sorry, sorry!"

I started reciting the alphabet to try and steady my thoughts. It took several minutes before it worked and I could feel him relax beside me.

"What were you thinking about?"

"My mother."

He stopped mid-stride and turned to face me. "Your mother? All of that was about your mother?"

"All of what?"

"Becca, you just launched about a hundred different emotions at me simultaneously. It was like warfare."

"I'm sorry! I was just thinking of her. I didn't even realize I was feeling anything, I swear!"

"How are you not suicidal?" he grumbled, but his touch was feather light against my cheek. "Do you want to talk about it?"

"I think you need rest. I'm used to my life. You are the one still trying to adjust."

"Yeah, no shit. Some other time then?"

I nodded and, for once, it wasn't just a delay tactic. I wouldn't mind talking to him about her. He said what he thought without being patronizing. He commanded me without threatening me. And he was unexplainable...just like her death.

"Do me a favor, will you?"

"Hm?"

"I know I put the suggestion of a tourist in your head but..."

I grinned. "I'm going home. Under guard. I will shower, climb into bed, and pleasure myself while remembering what it felt like...you know before you turned me down."

"Sassy, Becca," he chuckled. "I think she's my second favorite."

"Then who's the first?"

He nuzzled my neck. "The naked one."

✳⚔♯

Cael

What the fuck was I thinking? I wanted her more than I'd wanted anyone since becoming a Saint. It was primal how much I wanted her, how my body yearned to have her close. Her emotions were so raw, so persistent, that it reminded me of a time before this, a time when emotions were something to be felt rather than evaluated. Being reminded of the past was never smart...it made you long for things that were no longer possible. And Ethan, the closest thing I had to a real brother, needed me to take her. I cursed the gods above and below for choosing now to give me a fucking conscious.

"Watching the dawn alone? How unexpected."

"She is..." I trailed off, not wanting to admit he was right.

"Much more complex than a quick roll in the hay?" Ethan chuckled. "I believe, I-"

"Warned me, yes. Thank you. So why aren't you off with the lovely Sarah?"

"I took her home and gave her an archaic gentlemanly kiss before coming back."

"That's it?"

"We're meeting for coffee in a few hours before her shop opens." He shrugged. "Her safety was much more important than my own desires."

I turned to lean against the railing, facing him. "What does that mean? Did she not find you as irresistible as you hoped?"

"What the hell were you and Becca discussing or *doing* anyway?"

I gave him a withering glance. He knew better than to think I'd ever answer that question.

"Cael, you and Becca assaulted us tonight. Without warning, I might add. We were locked on a boat, a confined space, and the two of you were...well, your emotions were relentless. It was like a fucking hurricane lashing at us over and over. Every one of us is going home alone tonight. No one is trusting our own emotions right now."

I searched him, but he was bereft of feeling, as drained and exhausted as me. My eyes wandered over the men still circling on the dock below, the pallor of their eyes visible under the gas lights. Even from here, their weariness was obvious. I wasn't about to apologize so I said the only other thing that came to mind: "That seems dangerous."

Ethan nodded. "I've sent most of them back to the Row to recover. I didn't want anyone traveling alone."

"Has this happened before? Everyone weakened all at once?"

"Decades ago, long before my time. I've asked the journals be pulled so we can go through them later. Maybe they'll explain it or at least tell us how to protect against it."

I hated to doubt her, but I had to ask the question before it festered. "Was it intentional? Did she set out to weaken us?"

"No." His voice was strong, full of certainty. "Deception is not just an action; it's a betrayal. We would have sensed that. Besides, it was as much you as it was her."

I could hear the hesitation in his voice. "But?"

"But there are some things I should clarify. You wouldn't listen to me before but perhaps now you will. Take a walk with me to clear our heads?"

It wasn't a request but an order, and I stepped in line behind him. When we got to the dock below, he talked only briefly with the remaining men, sending them home for rest. They protested, not wanting to leave us alone, but he cut off their arguments fast and waved them on.

"You want privacy again," I guessed. "This is becoming a new side of you."

"Not new. It's only new that I trust you enough to bring you along."

I laughed. "So my running away made you trust me more? I'll have to remember that."

"It made me realize you're no longer a foundling that blindly follows orders simply to please his master."

"Harsh, that was harsh."

"But not unfair."

"No," I agreed, "not unfair. So where are we going?"

"To see your girl."

Lies. She had lied to me. She hadn't gone home. She had lied to me. Led me on, made me believe she would be in bed thinking of me. It was something I might do. Under other circumstances, I might even respect her for the audacity, but fuck...she lied to me.

Ethan's head rolled back in laughter. "Damn, brother, that was intense."

"She said she was going home," I groused.

He was still chuckling as he paused to grab a coffee from an early morning street vendor. He handed a cup to me before taking his own. "Don't pout. She went home, took a shower and got out of that unbelievable fucking dress. But she didn't stay. She doesn't sleep much, remember? I told you we catch her wandering the streets at all hours."

"She's in no condition to be wandering the streets."

"What do you mean?"

"She's unstable. It's the anniversary of her mother's death."

"I wondered about the change. Last night was totally off the mark for her. She usually walks around with a mug of chicory coffee not a fifth of cheap

Cuervo. I was beginning to worry it was your return affecting her. Glad to know it's something more mundane."

"She described it as brutal. Savage."

The tone of my voice was enough to dissolve his humor, and he shot a dark look my direction. "How long ago?"

"Just a year. Do you remember anything of it?"

"I know the death was unexpected, and I saw the inheritance papers during the background checks, but otherwise no. Considering the things she's seen in her job, if she calls it brutal, I would assume it should have been big enough to make our radar. I'll look into it. Are you stronger or do you need a few more minutes?"

"I'm good."

He urged me forward a few more blocks and then stopped us, leaning against a graffiti covered wall. He nodded across the street. "There's your girl."

I lifted my eyes to the second floor of the converted warehouse. Floor to ceiling windows illuminated the loft space, and I could see Becca sitting cross-legged on a table in the middle of the room. She lifted a slip of paper, a photograph I assumed, and studied it before taking a sip out of a mug and then repeating the process. She was so engrossed in her work that she seemed oblivious to anything else. Her moves were repetitive, almost hypnotic...

"For fuck's sake," Ethan growled. "Close your eyes."

"What?"

"Close your damn eyes! You can't even look at her without getting a hard-on. Silence your own thoughts for a minute, would you?"

I closed my eyes, fighting down the visions of Becca filling my head. I started to reach out, to try and figure out what he was showing me when it hit me: blackness, dark and suffocating; tears, fierce and impossible to stop; and something else, something undefinable that tore into my soul and dropped me to my knees.

My eyes flashed open, gulping shallow breaths to keep myself from vomiting. I struggled back to my feet, Ethan's strong hand steadying me. I closed my eyes again, this time searching out innocence and happiness to block out whatever had just surged through me. A few blocks away a child was playing in a puddle, stomping with abandon and completely oblivious to his parent's growing impatience. I held onto that, basking in it, as I waited for my heartbeats to settle. Then I whirled. "What the hell was that?"

"Compassion," he murmured. "And grief."

"I know grief."

Compassion was a bit dicier. We could sense compassion but not like normal humans...it was more an acknowledgment that it existed rather than a true emotion. It was self-preservation. You can't feel the depths of every person's pain in an entire city and not be affected. If we had human compassion running through us, we'd all be suicidal.

"Not like hers. For her, those two emotions are inexplicably intertwined. It's dropped every one of us to the ground so don't feel too bad."

"Yet another thing you failed to mention."

"And how, exactly, would I have explained it?" he spat. "By the way, Cael, there's this pretty average girl that's moved back to town. Normal life, normal upbringing, normal job, normal relationships but, oh yeah, her fucking *feelings* are strong enough to drop grown men to their knees? You would've had me committed."

"Point taken."

"Come on; there's something else."

He turned me the opposite direction, heading me toward the arts district. He stopped long enough to grab a postcard from a vendor and pass it my direction. It was a generic tourist card with a view of Saint Louis Cathedral.

"This time I will warn you."

I grimaced. "With a postcard? Is this a clue I'm meant to decipher? Do I look like a Hardy boy?"

"Look at it and tell me what you feel."

"Nothing. It's a piece of fucking cardstock, Ethan. It has no emotions. I may have been on an extended vacation, but it's not like I got my training yesterday."

I tossed the card into the gutter as he turned down an alley and rapped a few times on a steel door. Brilliant white light flooded over us as the door opened and, beyond, the modern glass and chrome signaled one of the newer art galleries. The guard greeted Ethan with a warm handshake and waved us in but, Ethan halted me with a solid hand in the center of my chest. "That postcard? Everything you thought you knew? It's all about to change."

We stepped into the gallery, and it was just like any other social event: a hundred different emotions flickering simultaneously. Like a hum in my head, white noise that was indecipherable until I chose to focus on something specific. I began to sort them out, one by one, the way I was trained. It's how we defined who was in true danger, who was deadly and remorseless, who would be an easy lay, and who was too high maintenance even to approach. Everyone's emotions were laid out for the taking if I could focus.

Love. Confusion. Fear. Contentment. Despair. Loneliness. Gratitude. Exhaustion. Peace.

It was a bizarre combination, yes, but not shocking and damn sure not cataclysmic. I opened my mouth to ask for an explanation when recognition dawned: the gallery was empty. A few employees were toiling in a work area upstairs focused on their tasks, and there was a man projecting greed - most likely the director, but otherwise it was vacant space. I glanced

around for a separate hall, a meeting room or recep-
tion area but there was nothing.

"Ethan-"

He tipped his chin toward the display pillars. "It's
the photos."

"No, that's-"

He gave a hiss of impatience. "It's the fucking photos."

I narrowed my eyes, disbelieving, and stepped to
the nearest exhibit. The black and white image would
draw an emotion from all but the most heartless of
viewers: a boy of five or six dressed in tattered jeans;
his rail-thin body dripping ocean water from the surf
behind him; grains of sand clinging to his face and
hair; his tiny hand outstretched to accept a blanket
from an unseen savior. The clarity was undeniable. Almost like an invisible tidal wave, a singular emotion
rushed over me and drowned out the others: hope.

"Khaled, an eight-year-old refugee," Ethan read the
description card, "arrives on the shores of Pozallo,
Sicily. Known for its censorship and poor educational
system, his parents attempted to escape from Libya
seven times in hopes of having a future for their only
son. When his parents were executed, Khaled hid on
a freighter and made the journey alone. On the day of
his arrival, Khaled had one dream for his future: to
hold a book of his own."

"Becca," I whispered. "This is Becca's. All of them."

"Yes."

"She captured emotion, true emotion, in a photo-graph. On an inanimate object." I sank onto the near-est bench. It was real. I could feel his hope deep inside as if it was my own. I knew it was real. But I still couldn't believe it.

Ethan dropped down beside me. "There are Wic-cans all over the city. Voodoo practitioners. Devil wor-shipers and a hundred other sects of magic that we've cataloged. Some with real abilities and some that are only imaginary. I've gone back and read through every single entry. There is nothing, not even a footnote or passing anecdote that would hint at this ability. It's not only unknown; it's inconceivable."

"Have you told anyone? Asked anyone?"

"No."

"Why?"

But he didn't need to answer. His emotions were so intense it was almost blinding: he feared for her safety. Feared what might happen to her if others were to learn of her talent. Where we had been given the ability to sense emotions in others, Becca had the ability to capture it, share it, make others feel it as if the emotions were their own.

"In the wrong hands-"

In the wrong hands, her talent was one dangerous fucking weapon. The ability to control someone's emotions, to define what hurt them, turned them on, made them sick or made them happy...that was a power reserved for gods, not humans.

"Does she realize-"

"No, how could she?" he asked, a visible shudder running through him.

"This is why you've had her followed, put safe-guards in place for her."

"Yes. I don't believe anyone knows yet, but I can't be certain. Just like everyone in this city, she is our responsibility, Cael. She's just...a bit more tiresome and dangerous for us all."

I could feel the exhaustion in his words, the weight he'd been carrying in my absence. Our world was tip-ping on its axis, and I'd left him alone to face it. My voice was stronger than I felt. "We'll take shifts, add more security at the Row, get through those journals. The answers exist somewhere."

He nodded and gave a last glance around the room. His eyes shifted a little, and he grimaced: Becca was nearby somewhere, and her emotions were more vi-brant than ever. "I've got to meet Sarah. You're good?"

I nodded. He might be unnerved by her emotions but, rather than danger, I only felt fascination. "I'll catch you later."

CHAPTER FOUR

Becca

I'd worked for hours but still couldn't get the Saint brothers out of my head. Sarah couldn't stop gushing about Ethan and, while I was glad she was so happy, my ability to fake merriment had been tested to its limit. As soon as she fell asleep, I was out the door to find solace in the quiet of my workspace. Going through the latest prints had helped, it gave me focus and time without my thoughts being invaded by Saints. I couldn't go anywhere in the city without one of the Saints appearing. Even when they tried to hide in the shadows, they were just always *there*. It was beginning to make me paranoid.

Sure enough, when I made a stop at the gallery to check on the upcoming exhibit, it didn't surprise me to see Cael and Ethan. Even with the gallery technically closed, they were sitting side by side; their heads dropped in deep discussion. They looked so serious that I sidestepped them into the office to find the director. We'd only spoken a few minutes before Cael joined us, a deep frown creasing into his chiseled features.

"You aren't sleeping."

I had expected to feel awkward in the daylight, to be wordless after his "non-rejection" last night but his directness washed it away. He was just as irrepressible as all of the Saints. I smiled and waved toward the director in introduction. They made small talk about fundraising and donations. Cael offered a sizable contribution without any preamble and then turned to me as if the director didn't exist.

"Have you had breakfast?"

"No. You?"

"Like you, I haven't even been to bed yet. Beignets?"

"Sarah and Ethan will be-"

"No beignets then. Chili omelets?"

My stomach growled at the mere mention of them. "God, yes. Please."

I gave the director a quick kiss on the cheek before taking Cael's arm and allowing him to lead me out.

"So is this what you do between fighting crime? Payoff gallery owners to get sneak peeks at upcoming exhibits?"

"Your work is...breathtaking."

I hesitated, unsure if he was sarcastic. "It's just photographs, not art, but thank you."

"And you are modest. Very few people are actually modest, you know. It's a front for their pride, but I can feel your blush rising. What book did you give him?"

"Pardon?"

"Khaled," he explained. "The little boy on the beach in Sicily."

"Oh, The Little Prince by Saint-Exupéry." I paused in my steps, eyeing him. "How did you know I bought him a book? I told no one about that, not even Sarah."

"It was his dream," he said with a shrug. "I don't envision you a person that would let that go unful-filled if it's within your power to control."

I accepted his tug forward but gave an exasperated huff. "It's unfair how well you know me already."

He laughed, light and airy, in total contradiction to his mood. "Ask me anything, Becca."

"Why such a foul humor today?"

"I grow weary of Ethan's overprotectiveness."

"Something we can agree on then."

He gave me a half smile. "In your case, it seems well founded. I am not nearly as fragile as you."

"Can you tell me about your family - the Saints?"

"Do you have plans this afternoon?"

"An appointment at four."

"After breakfast, perhaps we could take a walk somewhere less...," he considered his words a second before shrugging. "Just less."

I squeezed his arm. He wasn't telling me no. He was telling me that wasn't a conversation to be had in public. "Sounds fair. Just promise you won't distract me, and I miss my appointment."

"I can do quick," he chuckled.

Taking advantage of his lightened mood, I cut in front of him, running my hands over his chest as I continued to walk backward. "I don't want you to do quick."

His hands locked on my hips, keeping me from stumbling and smiled. "Mmm, so this is the sassy Becca Ethan warned me about."

"Does he warn you of everyone?"

"Only you."

My eyes flashed before I could prevent it and I stopped dead. "Did Ethan forbid you from me?"

"Anger," he laughed. "I've only know one other person ever to be angry with the venerable Ethan Saint."

"Who?"

He nuzzled my neck, before turning me to get me moving again. "Me."

"So did he?"

"Ethan forbids very little but he does offer his wizened counsel more often than any of us would like."

"That's a hell of a non-answer."

"So sassy. Feeling more your usual self today?"

"The sunshine keeps the darkness at bay," I admitted, "but feed me before the grumpiness returns."

He waved me into Camellia Grill, and we took the first seats we could find at the counter. He ordered for both of us and then slipped his fingers to intertwine with mine, resting them on his thigh. It was so easy, so comfortable. I tried to shutter away from the thought that he was here only to protect me at Ethan's bidding.

"So were you born here?"

He smiled, and I knew he was happy he could finally answer something. "No. I'm from New York originally. I only moved here after joining the Saints. I've been here...damn, fifteen years now."

"You joined as a teenager then. But you left and just now returned?"

"Ethan claims it was a rebellious phase. I took off trying to bury some things but leaving only made it worse."

"Something else you can't explain now. Got it. So, what can you tell me?" He frowned again, and I laughed. "Are you just now realizing how little of your life can be discussed in public?"

"Pretty much," he grimaced. "Safer topic: tell me how you got into photography."

"There are photos of me as a toddler carrying a Polaroid around my neck, so I've loved it pretty much forever. One year, Sarah and I were both given cameras for Mardi Gras. Just cheap disposable things, and we took them to a parade. We were standing shoulder to shoulder, taking our pictures, but when they were developed, you would never have guessed we were even at the same parade. I loved the idea of that, the mystery of it. Two people will never see the world the same way. When I take a photograph, I realize that I am pausing my life...it's a moment in time that no one could experience even if they were right beside me. It will never amount to anything more than my view, my choice, my emotion in that brief fraction of a second. And then I just hope that I can capture even a hint of what my subjects are truly facing, so they aren't forgotten."

I bit my lower lip, realizing I was rambling about something he probably didn't actually give a damn about. It was small, getting to know you, talk. Not some in depth analysis of my belief system regarding photography. I grabbed the chocolate shake in front of me and looked over at him.

As expected, he was staring off somewhere in the distance.

"Sorry," I mumbled. "I bored you already."

"No," he smiled and focused back on me. "Not at all. You actually answered something about your photos that fascinated me. Well, me and Ethan."

I tugged the straw out of my mouth as I choked a little. "Wait. Exactly how fucking often do you two talk about me?"

He grinned, and I could feel his guard drop the tiniest fraction. "Frequently. You were born here?"

I nodded but, deciding I wouldn't fall into that trap again; I kept my answer brief. "I went to college in New York, at Parsons, but moved back right after graduation."

"You lived in New York?"

"Long enough for school, yes. Can't picture me as a New Yorker?"

"No, not really."

"I couldn't either. That's why I'm back."

"But you travel a lot?"

"When duty calls, yes. I shouldn't say it like that. When something grabs my attention, I go. Often with little warning."

He chuckled. "That was a warning for me, wasn't it? That you might disappear without even a note?"

"I'd text. From the airport maybe."

"Please do. Your absence would send poor Ethan into a fit thinking you were kidnapped."

"He is...parental, isn't he? Oh, look! Saved by the omelet."

I dug in, just to keep my mouth from continuing to spout information. It took me a few minutes for me to realize he wasn't eating. "You don't eat? I thought that was a movie thing reserved for vampires."

"Do you believe in things like that? Vampires, ghosts, werewolves?"

"Why wouldn't I? Just because I haven't met any doesn't mean they don't exist. I hadn't met a man so vile he'd rape a hundred little girls in hopes of having a blonde haired heir until I went to the Sudan but it turns out he existed. Oh, God, don't tell me you are a vampire! I cannot live without the sunshine."

"No," he chuckled. "I assure you, I'm none of the above. 100% mortal with a few extras thrown in, that's all. My work would probably be much easier, and safer if did have some immortal gene to fall back on. Sarah's shop is here close, isn't it?"

The quick topic change caused me to glance his way and the increasing frown on his face set my every nerve on edge. "Yes. Is something wrong? Did something happen?" I tried to rise from my seat, but his hand grasped my thigh, holding me down.

"Sorry, no. Ethan is just enamored with her. It's nauseating. I mean, really nauseating." He took a huge bite of his omelet, swallowing it down with force. Then another. But now I could only pick at mine.

"I scared you. I'm sorry. Do you want to go check on her?"

"Please-"

He took another huge bite to finish the omelet off, then stood, and tossed a handful of bills on the counter. His hand went to my back, allowing me to lead. We were there in less than a minute but, until I had her engulfed in a hug, I still didn't breathe. I knew they all thought I was nuts, especially Cael and Ethan who were exchanging dark looks over our heads. I didn't care. She was safe. My sister was safe.

"Becca, honey-" Sarah's hand rubbed my head, pulling me a fraction away. Seeing the terror in my eyes, her eyes narrowed on Cael. "You," she hissed, "what did you-"

"I'm fine. It's fine. I just got spooked. You're good?"

"Perfect. Ethan's helping me open up. Not even a single customer yet. You sure-"

I felt stupid. Stupid and childish. And what made it worse was both of the men knew exactly what I was feeling. I couldn't even be embarrassed without them knowing.

Cael's fingers slipped to my hip, heavy and reassuring. "You're just exhausted, Becca. Let me take you home."

I nodded, hugging her again before letting him lead me away. She would be relentless in her questioning later but, thankfully, she let me keep some dignity when they were around. Too bad she didn't know they knew my every emotion and could help me figure out how to mend the choking embarrassment.

✴ ⚔ 𝄐

Cael

"Why are you embarrassed? I worry about the safety of every person in this damn city. Your concern for her is admirable."

She ignored me and waved around the house, a five-second tour of where every room was located. Then she hurried to the kitchen and began calling out what beverages she had to offer me. What an exasperating woman...protecting people is my job. How much clearer did I have to be?

I stepped into the kitchen, shutting the refrigerator and locking her body against it. "You were terrified. Ethan says trouble always finds you but is this something else? Are you expecting someone to come after you and Sarah?"

"Expecting? No."

"But?"

"But," she huffed, and I allowed her to break my grasp. "I wasn't expecting anything to happen to my mother either."

"Was it in the shop?"

She nodded but was stalking away from me. I followed her into her bedroom, sinking down on the edge of the bed. She was putting her hair up, kicking off her shoes...anything to avoid even looking my direction.

"You were there?"

"Yes."

Like pulling fucking teeth. "Why?"

"It was early morning. I went to help with a delivery, but when the knock came, it wasn't the delivery guys."

Now we were getting somewhere. "Where was Sarah?"

"Overseas on a purchasing trip."

Her hesitation would have told me something was off even if I couldn't read her emotions. "Wait. Does Sarah not know what happened to your mother?"

She shook her head but keep piddling around her room. I could not handle any more of her emotional riptide, and I stretched out on the bed. "Becca, come here."

She moved beside the bed, tears already filling her eyes. *Powerless.* She felt powerless, and I had no idea if it was due to the memories or my demand. My fingers grazed her waist, offering her the comfort of my touch. She climbed onto my lap, straddling my waist, and my hands locked on her hips to try and give her strength and reassurance. And then I understood: we had stalked her all over the city, taken lives in her presence, invaded her most private of emotions, and never once had any of the Saints bothered to explain shit to her.

"I'm not much of a scholar. I've never even read through our complete history, but I can tell you the basics. The Saints have been around since the founding of the earliest churches. They needed men willing to protect their people using any means necessary. They take us from a life that is a living hell and offer us redemption...the chance to make a difference, be a better soul, to become guardians that help and protect those who need it."

"Like a spiritual police force?"

"You could say that, yes. But none of us are innocent, Becca. We are deadly and make no apologies for it. When redeemed, we go through a rite, a ceremony, which gives us heightened senses. Or maybe we just learn to use them better than normal humans. We know our exact strength, how far we can push ourselves until exhaustion, how to cue into people's emotions. It's like holding a can of coffee in your hand. Even closed you can smell it but when you open it, the scent assaults you. That's what happens to all of our senses the moment the rite takes place. We have to train for years to learn to control them, distinguish them, make actual use of the abilities. Once we do, we go to work. We're assigned to places, and we spend the rest of our days fulfilling our redemption...making a difference in what can be a very shitty world."

I quieted as I read her emotions, waiting for her to have questions or fears or confusion. But my explanation had either barely registered, or she really had prepared herself to accept anything I told her. When she said nothing, I let my fingers trail against her delicate wrist, my voice a low hum.

"So what you need to understand right now is that this is my sole purpose for existing. Protecting you, protecting the others who call this city home, it's what allows me to live and breathe and walk on this earth. Needing me, or any of the guardians for that matter doesn't mean you're weak, Becca. It just means you're human. So, please, I *beg* you, trust that I am damn good at my job, take a deep breath, and let's start again. Okay?"

After only a few breaths, her emotions settled to something more manageable, and she nodded.

"Were they strangers?"

She didn't answer right away, but I knew, this time, it wasn't avoidance. She just didn't want to voice the truth.

"I still look for them on the street, in every dark alley I walk, but I didn't know them. I've tried to rationalize why she even opened the door but..."

"Your mother knew them?"

She nodded, and her body tensed as if it was going to curl into itself. I stroked her thighs, deep and slow until I could hear her heartbeat calm. "You know you're safe with me, right? I could sense anyone coming a half mile away. Whoever they are, you're safe right now, Becca."

"They argued, but it was very brief. The only part I remember was the very last...when she looked over at me and then turned to them and said *It was me. It was all me.* That was it. It was the last thing other than screams that came from her throat."

"What did she mean?"

"I've no idea." She shook her head and then began playing with the buttons on my shirt to avoid my gaze. "They beat her within an inch of passing out but left her conscious just enough to feel the rest of the pain they inflicted. They carved things into her, symbols, initials, markings...I don't even know how to describe them. They chanted some prayer over her, dusted her with something silvery that smelled like pine. It was a ritual of some sort, I know that, but it was no faith we subscribed to. Cael, it lasted hours. They tortured her, bled her out in her own shop, for hours. And I could do nothing but sit there, tied to a wooden pillar and beg them to stop. After a while, I begged them just to hurry and get it over with so she'd be in less pain. We'd gotten there at 4:08, a customer finally found us at 10:30."

She stopped to catch her breath and chanced a glance at me. Her emotions had taken their toll, my eyes were probably a terrifying storm of gray, and I silently thanked the heavens that there was no other Saint nearby to read them. There was a sympathetic physical pain for her mother's torture, pity for Sarah's lack of knowledge, hatred for those who committed such an act, and confusion over what the hell it meant. But, more blinding than anything was guilt: this had happened on our watch, in our town, to one of our own. While I'd been globetrotting like a cowardly fucking child afraid of his own shadow.

She leaned down, caressing my face, soothing kisses along each twitching muscle. I cupped her face in my hands, barely able to speak.

"We failed you, and there are no apologies that can ever change that."

"We're all only human, remember?" she whispered. Her lips were soft against mine, salty tears trickling down and infusing me with her heartbreak.

It was undeserved forgiveness, an unwarranted reprieve that I couldn't accept. I returned her kiss with a longer, deeper, more selfish one of my own. Then I moved her to lay beside me, cradling her tiny body into mine as if I could actually protect her. "Sleep, Becca. Right now, I need you to sleep."

I fought sleep, trying to piece through what happened to her mother and protect her at the same time. But it was impossible. I was as shattered as she. It was hours later, the sun almost touching the horizon when Ethan's violent grip finally pulled me awake. I jerked up, slinging sweat everywhere and he lurched backward.

"Cael-"

I clutched my head, rocking myself, a collision of emotions flooded through me. *Worry. Concern. Guilt. Fear...so fucking much fear.*

"Leave us," he ordered, his voice a quiet hum in my head. I heard shuffling, doors shutting and then, blissfully, only Ethan's emotions. He sank down on the bed, his hand on my head. "Better?"

I nodded, shaking him off. I stood up, moving to the bathroom to splash water on my face.

When I came back, the quiet was unnerving, and I went to the door, letting my hand hover over the

wood. It took me a few tries before I found the etching. "Did you put the rune in?"

"Not my strength but I didn't have a lot of choices.
It's crude, I know, but effective enough."

"When?"

He knew that wasn't really the question I was ask-
ing. "You've been screaming for three hours."

"And Becca?"

"Safe, unharmed. Refused to leave your side despite
my urging to the contrary. She told me she didn't care
if I carved a fucking pentagram on her door if it would
ease your torment. That's a direct quote, by the way."

"The fear was Sarah's then."

"And my own," he admitted. "Tell me something
here, brother."

As I relayed the events of her mother's death, as my
mind provided its own torturous visions to the tale,
my fury continued to rise. By the time I'd finished,
Ethan had moved across the room from me to try and
put distance between us. I knew my emotions were
assaulting him, but I also knew he was capable of
weathering that storm. A stronger person, someone
like him, would have tried to temper themselves but I
didn't really give a damn. Ethan could describe any
traumatic event with chilling emotional detachment,
but I was not so disciplined. When he finally felt my
fury settle into something more ominous, he motioned me to take a seat and then sank across from
me.

"Cael."

He knew the murderous emotions raging inside me and his even, almost conciliatory tone, was infuriating. My eyes narrowed, my voice a low threat. "If I find out that one of our own..."

"I doubt-"

"You doubt, but you don't know."

"No, I don't," he admitted. "But I will find out. Guardians aren't the only ones to use runes. They've been used since the dawn of time with both good and bad intent. You said her mother knew the men. It could be she was involved in something that Becca had no knowledge of. It's New Orleans for chrissakes; anything is possible."

"So we find out."

"Yes, we will. Together. All of us. But, until then-"

"Do not ask me to walk away from her. I will not walk away after what she's been through, after having failed her already, after what we may have..." I trailed off, realizing I was close to yelling at him again. "You do not have that authority over me."

"No, I don't, but I can keep her out of the Row. You know how I feel about both her and Sarah, but I cannot put all the Saints in danger-"

"The danger to us is questionable at best, Ethan," I spat.

His calm demeanor vanished in a breath, and he lurched to his feet to tower above me. "No, it's not! Have you not realized your blackouts, the dreams that are so dark the devil might as well be calling for you himself, started just before her mother was attacked? And now, exactly a year later, when you meet the daughter that can turn all our emotions on end, they have suddenly reappeared? We have no explanation for any of that, Cael, and until we do-"

No. I hadn't put that together and fuck him for being so damn observant. I wanted him to protect her but, instead, he was determined to protect me. I wanted to hate him for it but couldn't. I dug my fists deep in my pockets to keep from accidentally strangling him. "I will not bring her to the Row."

"Cael, it's only temporary. We *will* find answers. For you, for her, for all of us. I promise."

CHAPTER FIVE

Cael

Ethan called Becca to the room but grabbed her arm before she could get far. "You need-"

"I don't need instructions, Ethan," Becca grumbled as she angled passed him. "Go be clairvoyant with Sarah."

"We're not-" he started but then shook his head. "Never mind. Just call if anything else-"

"Ethan, you love him, and you're worried. I get it, but he's a Saint, not a five-year-old."

I couldn't help the dark chuckle that escaped as he scurried away. Damn she knew how to put him in his place. I lifted my eyes, surveying her emotions, but she seemed calm. "I fear I've complicated your life in a single afternoon."

"Guilt and responsibility weighs heavy on you Saints, doesn't it?" she asked coolly. "We mere humans have pretty dark dreams, too. Mine, as you well know, happen to come when I'm awake."

"Becca-"

She sank into my lap, not waiting for the permission she knew I wouldn't give.

My every muscle had turned to stone. I'd gone to sleep with her in my arms and then had been blindsided with terrorizing nightmares, soul-searing visions that I couldn't define, and then Ethan's damned observations. Too much had changed too quickly for me to settle my adrenaline. Yet, she didn't seem to care. Her touch was as exploring and confident as before. Fearless. I tried again. "Becca-"

"I'm not afraid of a few bad dreams, Cael. If you expected me to be scared and run, you don't know me as well as you think. Yes, this has turned out to be more complicated than a quick Frenchman Street hookup. But, let's be honest, we realized that the moment you first touched me in the alley, didn't we?"

"Yes."

"It's why you keep stopping us."

"Yes."

"If you want me to leave, I'll leave," she offered.

I should be noble. I should turn her down. But even Saints fall. "I don't want you to leave."

She leaned into me, her lips sweeping soft against mine. Her hand cupped my cheek, loosening my resolve with each tender stroke of her thumb. My lips parted, bringing her deeper, my tongue seeking hers in a desperate attempt to connect with every unseen part of her. I knotted my hands in her hair, clinging to her strength.

She pulled a heartbeat away, her voice so quiet I wasn't sure if she actually spoke the words, or I merely felt them. "And will you stop me now?"

"No. Yes. No."

My indecision gave her the only opening she needed, and she did a slow shimmy to kneel at my feet. Her fingers stroked a tender path up my thighs as she took hold of my belt and began to loosen it.

I had always preferred hard, fast and relentless...until her. There was no timidity in her strokes, her hands and mouth working together to coax me to hardness. Her patient moves were as bewitching as they were seductive and, with absolute dazzling clarity, I realized how her talent worked: she could make the world disappear not only for herself but for the subjects in her photographs. Their lives, their emotions, were captured because at that singular moment nothing else existed...she could make you forget every pain, every heartbreak, even death if she so desired. She allowed nothing to invade her desires, I remembered, and right now she desired nothing more than to ease my torment and lift me from the darkness holding me captive.

I was using her for a comforting power she didn't even realize she possessed. Her languid movements were keeping me locked in a haze where nothing else existed. It was impossible, unexplainable, and danger-ously addictive. I didn't want her like this. I didn't want to use her as a comfort or escape. I didn't want to use her, period, but my body allowed for no dis-tinction.

I willed my body not to come, but it was useless. I was under her command, and she knew what I needed more than me. I tried to distract myself, but she was blocking everything, leaving me nothing to focus on except the soft cushion of her mouth against the stiff-ness of my cock. As I felt the spasms rising, I tossed up silent prayers in a last effort to stay here in this tranquil place she created. Something in my de-meanor gave my emotions away, and she grasped my hand, lacing our fingers together at my waist.

Her tongue continued to flick me, even slower now, and her lips traced along the edge of my cockhead. My orgasm came long and subdued, as dark and heavy as southern molasses, a silent river that she swallowed down even as she continued to suck me off. It was the quietest orgasm I'd ever experienced, and the only one that had ever left me heartbroken after.

She was too strong. Whatever its origins, this tal-ent, this power of hers, could enslave any man and destroy every Saint. We endanger her...she endangers us. It's an impossible liaison.

I didn't bother to zip my pants and pulled her off the floor, crushing her into my arms. Her fingers were on my face, stroking, caressing, evaluating my mood.

"Cael-"

"In a world of maddening chaos, you tether me to a reality I fear more than anything."

"I fear nothing."

"That," I managed, "is dangerous for us both."

Becca

When I was seventeen, I'd made a joke about marriage to a guy I was dating. The word alone sent him running to the bathroom where he proceeded to lose his lunch. Cael had that same look now - like he couldn't wait for the first opportunity to flee. And yet, he stayed. We were doing nothing except sitting around the room watching reports of the storm heading our way. After a brief chat with Ethan, he'd joined me on the couch, snuggling me close to him. It was as if he was torn between running and never leaving my side.

For as much as I wanted to make him better, though, it was Sarah that had my stomach tied in knots. She seemed infinitely happy in Ethan's arms but, whenever she thought we weren't looking, a melancholy air enveloped her.

"It's not Ethan. It's sadness," Cael murmured in my ear, "and loneliness. For family, I assume."

I squeezed his arm in thanks.

"Now it's my turn to offer: if you want us to leave, we will."

"I get the impression that Ethan will never allow us freedom from bodyguards."

"Of course not but they'd be stationed outside." His palm moved to my thigh, giving me a single, brief squeeze. "You worry that we're only here for guard duty. I can't blame you. I'm not sure how to assure you that we do go off duty and enjoy ourselves-"

"I know you enjoyed yourself," I cut in, grinning.

I was rewarded with a warm chuckle, and his eyes started to regain their usual gleam. "Let me just say that, at least where the bedroom is concerned; we don't do obligation. We are both here because we choose to be. We could assign someone to watch you, but that wouldn't be nearly as much fun as having you get dressed up and taking you both out for a night on the town so we can all unwind. What do you say we try it and go from there?"

"I have a better idea." I whistled to Ethan to draw his attention from my sister's lips. "Do you own a car?"

"Several."

I ignored the arrogant smirk he sent me. "Can you leave the city limits?" I frowned, not sure what story he'd given to Sarah about their crime fighting tendencies. "I mean, are you on duty or call or whatever-"

"Depends entirely on whether or not your plan is something I want to do," he chuckled. "I get enough violence in my day job. If you're going to traipse me through a war-ravaged jungle with Columbian drug lords, then I'll pass."

"I turned that down, thank you very much."

"Wait, what?" Cael tensed beside me. "That was a consideration?"

"Sarah mentioned it earlier," Ethan explained. "And we are all quite thankful you passed on that assignment." He ruffled my hair as he walked past with Sarah trailing right behind.

"I was worried she'd accept," Sarah admitted. "She's such an escapist sometimes. What do you have in mind?"

"A road trip. Where the saltwater will cling to your clothes, the beer colder than icebergs, and the seafood straight off the boat."

Sarah's face lit up, and she bounced on her toes. "Seriously, Becca? Do you have time? I mean, can we do that?" She whirled, catching Ethan in the chest. "You're too busy, aren't you? It's not like-"

His hand wrapped around her waist. "Anything that makes you that fucking happy with only a cryptic clue isn't something I could ever say no to."

"Whipped. My brother is whipped," Cael groaned.

"We'll run to the Row, get cleaned up and pick you up in a half-hour or so?"

Sarah nodded and started bestowing thankful kisses on his neck. I shook my head. "That's my cue for a shower as well, I think."

Cael hooked his thumb into my belt loop to follow behind, his eyes still intent on Ethan and Sarah. When we made it to my room, he gave a visible shudder. I turned, automatically on guard.

"What is it?"

"Sarah is a very affectionate creature, isn't she?" he asked, gathering up his things from my room.

I laughed, relaxing. "Much more than me. Sorry if that's what you are looking for."

"I wasn't looking for anything, and yet I found you." He stepped toward me, tucking his arms around my waist. "Your appointment this afternoon. The one I made you miss. Columbian drug lords?"

"Yes, but don't get that guilty look on your face. I would never leave her this week."

"No, I don't imagine you would," he murmured. "Do you ever intend on telling her?"

"No. Giving her graphic visuals of our mother's death is cruel."

"You've buried this inside for a year-"

I could hear the judgment etched in his words, and I grimaced. "Never, Cael. I'll never tell her."

"You shouldn't have to face this alone, Becca."

I broke away from him, tugging fresh clothes out of my armoire. "I'm not. You know, which means Ethan knows, which means every Saint in this stupid city knows. My bigger concern is trying to get you guys to keep your mouth shut."

"Sarah can-"

"Not handle it," I interrupted, leveling a hard gaze at him. "She has her very own history, Cael, and she is not strong enough to have these images in her head. Ask Ethan. He has her every emotion cataloged and will tell you the same thing."

"I don't need to ask Ethan. I believe you, and I promise she'll never learn of it from one of us."

I nodded and stepped away, moving to the doorway. Stretching to tiptoes, I let my fingers trace over the design Ethan had etched on the frame.

"It's a protective spell. A rune," he explained. "It blocks out emotions from those on the opposite side."

I nodded again and hugged the clothes to my chest. I knew it was an obvious defensive maneuver he would pick up on instantly, but I couldn't seem to contain it. My every move was allowing him further insight even when I was trying so hard to block him out.

"I'm on this side with you, Becca," he mumbled. "And you are growing darker by the second so please just ask."

I refused to turn, refused to give him more. But my words tumbled out unbidden. "I don't want to know the answer."

"You fear nothing, remember?" His voice was harsh and demanding...a clear challenge.

"It's like the marks on my mother," I whispered.

"Yes. I guessed that from your description."

I was unable even to guess at the emotion that colored his voice. "Did Saints do this to her?"

"Ethan would never have sanctioned-"

"That's not what I asked."

He exhaled, long and heavy. "No, it's not. But right now it's the only answer I have."

It took several moments for me to turn and face him, my spine straightening, my voice resolved. "Cael, if I find out this was a Saint, you need to understand..."

My response apparently caught him off guard because he rushed to my side, his hands digging hard into my arms. "No. You need to understand. If it was a Saint, they have chosen to play God. They are traitors of the lowest form imaginable, and I *will* kill them myself."

His fierce promise should have frightened me. It would terrify any normal person but, sooner or later, I was going to have to face facts: my life is anything but normal. Instead, I felt an odd sense of relief.

"I don't deserve gratitude, Becca."

I offered him a half smile. "Accept it anyway."

"No."

"Yes."

He shook his head and gave me a forced smile. "Impossible, sweetheart, you are impossible."

CHAPTER SIX

Becca

The hour long drive down the coast would have been unbearable if not for Sarah's banter. She wasn't oblivious to the tension, but she had an amazing way of keeping things light and humorous. She'd curled as close to Ethan as possible in the front seat but would throw comments and jokes at us over her shoulder. I had always viewed them as the guardian/parental type figures but, watching them whisper and laugh in each other's ears; they seemed more like lovesick teenagers. I could only imagine what emotions the two of them were radiating, but poor Cael was fidgeting in the seat beside me. Anyone else might not notice, but I could feel the tension starting to draw through his every muscle. In return, Ethan's eyes flashed Cael's direction in the rearview mirror.

The two of them were so mercurial, able to go from happy to glowering in a single breath. I suppose if I had an entire city's emotions threading through me,

I'd be the same way. Afraid Cael would ruin Sarah's mood, and Ethan would start analyzing me in the interim, I decided the best approach was also the most inappropriate: making out with Cael in the back seat of the convertible. I'd expected him to try and dissuade me but, instead, he whispered "so mischievous" before locking his lips onto mine. Sarah loved every minute of it: the sexual frustration radiating from Ethan was thick enough to guarantee she would have a wild night ahead. Ethan was nearly blind with fury.

When we finally arrived at the rough, weather-beaten pier house, Ethan lurched from the car, his palms resting on his knees as he tried to catch his breath. Sarah was at his side, and he mumbled something about being carsick to try and fend off her concern.

He whirled on us, and we offered him the most innocent looks we could manage.

"I am never speaking to you two again."

"Promise?"

"Becca Riley! Tell me you didn't steal that car!"

I glanced up to find the voice, seeing him outlined in the restaurant's door frame. "Billy!" I dashed up the rickety stairs and hopped into his open arms.

"The gorgeous Becca has stopped traveling the world to grace us with her presence. Hide the Crimson Voodoo, boys, before she drinks it all!" He twirled me around before setting me back on the dusty floor.

"Once! I drank you out once."

"Once is all it takes to make history, Becca. Tell me Sarah's with you."

I waved my hand behind where Cael and Ethan were taking seats at one of the long, wooden picnic tables that spanned across the open porch. As soon as Sarah had them seated, she stepped forward, slower and with more grace than I could ever exhibit. I moved back to the men and let her take my place in Billy's arms. His touch was soft on her face, brushing away tendrils of hair as he drank her in. Ethan's body gave a visible shudder and Cael straightened in his chair. I wrapped my arms around Ethan's neck, resting my chin on his shoulders to watch them.

"Relax, big brother," I chuckled. "That's her father."

Cael's head dropped back in laughter, and I knew my intuition had been right: Ethan had been ready to kill him.

"Becca, you are such a little shit," Ethan hissed.

I laughed. "Beer or bourbon?"

"Beer," they answered in unison.

I strode inside over to a nearby chest cooler, pulling out Crimsons for everyone and popping them open before moving back. I handed them out and then took a seat on the tabletop as Sarah and her father continued to catch up in soft voices.

"You said her father," Cael prompted. "You have different fathers?"

"I assumed you Saints had an inch-thick file on me by now. Yes, different fathers."

They exchanged a look, and I huffed. "Stop. Not tonight. You can't do that judging, evaluating shit tonight. Cael, you said it yourself: Sarah needs her family. Not whatever dark, mysterious goings on you two are debating. Please, let her be happy. I know you can tell she is."

I looked from one to the other, my voice pleading. "Please, she needs this. Even if just for one night."

Cael smiled. "And so do you."

"Agreed." Ethan swallowed down half his beer. "Now give me a shot of bourbon and introduce me to this man that may be my future father-in-law."

I choked on my beer. "You can do that? I thought the Saints were eternal bachelors."

"You've terrified her, Ethan," Cael laughed. "Becca thought she had a one-night stand guaranteed, and now you've fucking terrified her. Smooth move."

"Your issue, not mine. Becca?"

I narrowed my gaze at him. "You can be such an ass. Sarah! You're neglecting your *lover* over here. Maybe an introduction?"

"You will pay," Ethan hissed but winked at me as he left to join them.

I kicked off my sandals and tucked my feet onto Cael's legs. "He loves her?"

"Since the moment he saw her," he said nodding. "Never seen anything like it before in my life. I'd almost think him bewitched."

"Much more my mother's approach than Sarah's. She loves him too, I think. He makes her happy and safe anyway. It just seems fast."

"Saints have learned that 'waiting and seeing' is a useless human pursuit. Things are either right, wrong or somewhere in between. It rarely changes."

"Becca! You two want the special before the crowd hits?" Billy called. "Sarah isn't feeding this boy enough."

I nodded. "We'll grab some beers and walk the docks. Just give us a yell when it's ready."

Cael paused at the cooler, tucking a couple of bottles in one hand while guiding me with the other. "Specials?"

"They'll cover the table with newspaper and give you more seafood than you can ever consume."

"I have a very big appetite," he joked. "Fresh off the boat, I take it?"

I tilted my head to where boats were tying up. "A hole in the wall, yes, but the best food you've ever eaten."

"Don't let the calligraphy and engraved invitations fool you. We're all pretty simple creatures."

"Creatures?" I waved him toward one of the fishing piers that stretched over the bay waters. "What happened to humans? Are you going to grow tentacles or something?"

He grinned. "I meant men, not the Saints. Men are simple creatures."

"Sex, booze, and violence. Yep, pretty easy to navigate."

"But, yes, we are human. Just, you know, better."

"And arrogant."

"Yep and not about to apologize for it," he laughed. "So this is the closest you have to home, isn't it?"

I nodded and sank at the edge of the pier, letting my feet dangle off the end. "What gave that away?"

"Less darkness, more tranquility." He dropped to sit beside me. "And the smiles that I imagine are rare this week."

"True. All true." I smiled before angling my bottle his direction to get him to open it. He popped it off with one thumb and handed it back. "Built in bottle opener. I may have to keep you around."

"I can protect you with the strength of a thousand generations, kiss you until you can't breathe, and you want a bottle opener. You are the most bewildering woman I've ever met."

"Honest to a fault," I offered.

"There is that," he chuckled. "Tell me about Billy."

"He's run this place since his father died. He was sixteen, maybe? This is an institution to locals. He tried to fix it up once, had these grand plans for new paint, windows, interior freezers. There was this comical riot that ensued. A bunch of old, drunk, fishermen staged their version of protest by putting their entire catch on his porch and refused to clean it up until Billy agreed to leave the place unchanged. It didn't take too many days in the Louisiana heat for him to give in."

"You love him," he guessed. "Such fondness in your voice. What happened between him and your mom?"

I gave a half shrug. "I'm not sure how they met, only how they ended. Billy doesn't like to talk about her." I shook my head and took a long draft from the bottle. "He tried to be my father. He wanted the job at least. But that's not a job I'd wish on anybody. I am a handful, I think."

"Ethan would agree."

"And you?"

"I love a challenge, remember?" he murmured. "Did their split have anything to do with your mother bewitching people?"

I toyed with the edge of the bottle label, trying to figure out what I'd said or felt that allowed him that window into my thoughts. "Just a phrase, Cael."

"Why don't I believe you?" He nudged me with his hip. "You're willing to believe in werewolves but not that your mother could cast spells? Interesting double standard."

"Am I talking to Cael or a Saint?" I asked, my voice quieter.

"I wish I could tell you differently, but I am both. At all times."

"I like to imagine her the one part of my life that is normal. Until her death, I believed that to be true and now, I cling to it. Irrational, I know."

"You judge yourself so harshly. We all cling to things that give us hope." Cael kissed my head then unwrapped my fingers from the beer bottle to entwine them with his own. "You don't like talking about her either, do you?"

"Not really, no."

"To me or just anyone?"

"Anyone but you especially," I admitted.

"Becca-"

"I know you protect the city, its people, that you see and feel the absolute worst of humanity. Yes, it may help people and make them feel better, but despite what you say, I know that affects you somewhere deep inside that you don't allow anyone to see. I do not want to add to that burden."

"You're worried about me? Seriously? That's..."

"Ludicrous? Ridiculous? Childish? I don't care. Call it what you want, it's a boundary I've drawn for myself where you are concerned." I couldn't help the defensive tone in my voice. "You seem to approve of those."

"Sacrificial, Becca. I was going to say sacrificial."

"Everything okay down here?" Ethan's hand was heavy on both of our shoulders. "Because it doesn't feel okay from where I am."

"Deep, meaningful conversations," I sighed.

His eyes focused on Cael. "I thought we agreed on none of that tonight?"

"I need more alcohol to drown out her emotions," he grumbled. He leaned over and gave me a quick kiss before standing up. "And I'm off to find just that. Ask her about her mother, the witch, or how she won't confess to me because she'd rather put herself through hell rather than see me hurt."

He hissed the last word as if it was the most offensive word ever created and my eyes shot to Ethan's in confusion.

"Cael-" Ethan tried.

"See me after a few shots, deal?" He strode off without waiting for an answer and Ethan sank to take his place beside me.

"If someone doesn't trust that we can protect them, it calls into question everything we stand for. It's frustrating. Hurtful even."

I frowned. I *hurt* him? Cael was so cavalier about everything that I didn't realize that was even possible. "I never said..."

"If you don't trust him with words, how could you ever trust him with your life?" Ethan asked quietly. "Don't worry; we are very persistent. He'll have a few drinks, regroup and then try again. It's who we are."

"At the house, his dreams...they were so dark, so visceral. I don't want to add to that."

Ethan turned to face me, and I knew he was evaluating every emotion floating through me. I didn't care. If he did end up with Sarah, I wanted him to know exactly what I was feeling...even the ones I was still uncertain of.

"Oh, we are dealing with something totally different than I thought." He gave me a tender smile, tucking my hair out of my face and behind my ear. "He doesn't comprehend love and sacrifice, Becca. His life before was darker than most and neither of those were things he received. He's offended by your attempt to protect him because he thinks it means he failed. Think of it like someone taking a war assignment away from you. They take it away to protect you, but you would see it-"

"As a sign, I'm a tiny weak woman who can't handle it."

"Exactly. But, Becca, if there is anyone with the patience and tenacity to make him understand, I've no doubt it's you."

"Patience is not one of my strong suits," I reminded.

"I think you will surprise even yourself. Now, about your mother-"

"Growing up, gossip around the Quarter said she was a witch. Sarah's father believed in it enough to sever all ties. I didn't believe. I refused to believe."

"There's a difference there but you know that, don't you?"

I nodded. "I know you've been watching me for ages, Ethan. Surely you know all this."

"Actually, I don't. I admit the Saints have done a thorough job looking into your background, but there was nothing to indicate you and Sarah have different fathers and no gossip about your mother."

My forehead crinkled as I considered. "Doesn't that seem...fishy?"

"It seems," he hesitated, "orchestrated. For whatever reason."

I bristled. "You think that I-"

"No. I wondered for a while, I admit. Your history slowly coming to light, your continuing appearance at the most dangerous times. It made everything suspect. But I've learned that's not who you are. So, I'll keep looking and trying and investigating until I have answers. And I *will* get answers, Becca."

He stood up and pulled me to my feet. "Now, let's go raid the bar before Cael drinks it all. Deal?"

✳ ⚔ ⚓

Cael

I'd managed to down enough drinks to bury the childish frustration Becca had invoked but not nearly enough to join in the jovial dinner conversation. Sarah, bless her, tried everything to get me out of my foul mood. She even offered to dance on the table once the local band started tuning up. Ethan was pretty pissed I turned that one down. The way she was celebrating with her father, though, I figured the last thing she needed was more incentive to drink. I couldn't decide if she was drowning something of her own or just trying to unwind. Ethan didn't seem concerned, so I assumed Becca was right, and he was more in tune with her emotions than I. Either that, or I was too damned self-absorbed to recognize anything.

Even Becca's emotions were almost indecipherable. But only almost. She smiled, she laughed, she danced with both Billy and Ethan, but she had curtailed her drinking, and one single emotion surrounded her: I had put her on the defensive. The more I stared at her, the more it blossomed into a full-fledged shield that enrobed her, and I scowled. Before Ethan could corner me, I threaded through the growing crowd of locals and to the bar in the back. Ignoring the barkeep, I moved straight to the cash register and began trying to pry it open. I straightened, feeling her behind me before I even saw her.

"Robbing the cash register?"

"Billy won't let me pay for dinner or all the liquor I've consumed. You humans can be so damned charitable it's sickening."

"Yes," she laughed. Tight and tense like we were strangers. "Charity does have a nasty humanity to it, doesn't it?"

"That's not what I-"

"Yes, you did."

"Okay, I did. You're all so frustrating."

She waved off the kid behind the bar, and he disappeared before she even lowered her hand. "Do you always talk in generalities when you're drunk or are you just avoiding admitting you're pissed at me?"

"Both." I sighed and placed both hands on the counter to steady myself. I felt more human than I'd ever felt in my life. Conflicting emotions were racing through both my head and my cock and leaving me in some unsettling void where I couldn't think clearly much less do my job. At the same moment I hated her for it, I realized I was desperate for it as well. "Why must you be so obstinate?"

Her frozen features dissolved and she hesitated. "I don't mean to be."

It was true. I knew she wasn't being difficult on purpose. It's my job to protect people, but I can't say it's something I actually want to do. Ingrained, like breathing, but not some grand self-righteous gesture: it's a job, an obligation. But she wanted to protect the world, including me. Deep down in her confused naïve little soul, she believed in saving people. Maybe that's why she and Ethan understood each other so well, and I couldn't figure out either fucking one of them. They are good, and I'm...essentially not.

"I know that," I managed. "I get it. You're fearless. You need no one. Not even Saints."

She heard what I didn't say: *not even me.* She stepped closer; her fingers light on my arm as if I would jerk away.

"I know you think I'm strong," she whispered. "If I believe the town gossip about my mom- if I believe her a witch - then I have to admit she chose that life over Sarah's father. She let Sarah grow up without this amazing man because of her selfishness. And I have to acknowledge that her death was likely her own doing rather than a random act of violence. I am strong, Cael, but I'm not ready to be that strong. I'm sorry."

And suddenly it all made sense. She wasn't just protecting me...she was protecting herself from things she wasn't ready to face. The dark place that existed even when she was happy. She wasn't afraid...she was avoiding what she knew was inevitable. And that, I couldn't fault anyone for.

I turned to face her, surprised at the heartbreak written across her face. This crazy, fiery, frustrating woman was near tears because I'd cornered her. How had I not felt that? What a fucking dick.

"I'm sorry for being an ass. You turn me inside out, and I can't decide if that's good or bad." I leaned in, giving her a lingering whiskey scented kiss. "I only know it's something my life neither as a human or a Saint prepared me for. So bear with me, okay?"

She gave me a half smile. "Keep kissing me like that, and you've got a deal."

I pulled her into me, pressing my lips back into hers in a deep, truthful promise. "You forgive so easily. Even when it's unwarranted."

"Forgiveness is never unwarranted, Cael. Shouldn't Saints know that more than anyone?"

"You're more a saint than I could ever be, do you know that?"

A surge of adrenaline coursed through me with such force that Becca had to grab me to keep me upright.

"Well, you won't be driving back," she laughed, but I couldn't even manage a smile her direction.

"Everything okay?" Ethan's voice was light, but his hand was heavy on my shoulder, steadying and calming me without words.

"Damn, Ethan," she hissed. "Are we projecting too much anger, or frustration or heaven forbid lust? Can't you turn yourself off even for a little bit?"

"No, I can't. But, actually, it was too quiet. With you both involved, calm is a frightening emotion to contemplate."

"Kiss my ass, Ethan."

He nodded toward the opposite side of the room. "Sarah's about to pass out, and Billy wants to talk to you before we go."

She nodded. "Don't let him fall over, okay?"

"Babysitter on duty. Got it."

His grip tightened, his eyes flashing at me as soon as she was gone. "What the hell-"

"Can a Saint transfer their powers?"

"How much have you had to drink?"

I fought down the alcohol haze to let the full force of my emotions bear down on him. When the urgency in my head hit him, he gripped the bar top to steady himself, and his eyes darkened to midnight. "Yes. During wars, men dying on the battlefield tried transferring their powers to others. But the new ones were untrained, assaulting by emotions that weakened them rather than giving them strength. As noble the attempt, it was a complete failure."

"Do you have to be dying?"

"Why else would you-" Ethan cut himself off with the strangling look I sent him. "I imagine the ritual would be the same whether facing death or not, but I've never heard of anyone trying."

"Can Saints be born?"

He straightened, his eyes darting to Becca and then back to me. "Cael-"

"Can they?"

"Our powers are bestowed not inherited." He frowned, and I could sense the conflict raging through him.

"But?"

"Well, technically, again, the spells would be the same. Theoretically, a Council elder could bestow powers on a newborn or, yes, even a child in utero. In theory, it's possible, but it would be pointless. They would have no humanity instilled in them yet."

"Or," I hissed, "one could argue that an innocent child has more humanity than us all."

"Cael, what you're suggesting is-"

"Implausible, yes, but don't say impossible. Her abilities are different but not unrelated. It's no more impossible than a woman's grief being so powerful it can drop grown Saints to their knees or photographs that can command a man's free will."

Ethan stepped to me, close enough I could feel his breath hot on my chest. "A Saint that went outside the Council. An elder that went around every safeguard in place. You are talking betrayal, Cael."

He was warning me to tread very, very carefully and I nodded. "Maybe, maybe not. Becca told me that the last words her mother spoke were *It was me, it was all me.*" What if it was all her? Assume for a minute that her mother had the same ability to influence emotions. If she changed his will, made a Saint believe he should transfer his powers...you said it yourself, we have no way to protect against that type of magic."

"If they were hunting her mother because of your theory, because someone on the Council found proof any of this is true or even believed it possible..." he let out a long hiss. "They will protect themselves, *us*, at any cost. The danger to Becca is immeasurable. Cael, we *have* to find out who her father is."

Ethan was on the phone the moment we stepped out of the restaurant. His soft voice was inaudible, but his body language was clear enough: he was in mission mode. Ordering and commanding and having things readied for our return to the Row. I didn't even know where to start looking for answers, but he at least had some sort of plan swirling in his head.

"Little help?" Becca begged, struggling under the weight of her sister as she exited the building.

I scooped Sarah up and took her to the car, trying to shut out her drunken emotions. Damn she loved Ethan. How could this possibly end well for any of us? I tucked her into the front seat, glad when she passed out the moment I stretched her into the car. Becca's eyes drifted to Ethan only once before climbing in the back seat. I followed and, as soon as I was seated, she stretched out, resting her head in my lap and letting her feet dangle over the door edge.

"I told Billy I would run and check on his family before the storm rolls in. Will you take Sarah to the Row with you?"

Trusting us with her sister's safety? Not normal Becca. "Pardon?"

"I want her safe."

"What's changed to make you think she's not safe with you?"

She waved her bare foot Ethan's direction. "He doesn't think she is and that's good enough for me."

"What makes you assume-"

"I'm not an idiot so don't treat me like one," she murmured. "She'll be safe there, right? You promise me, Cael."

My hand cupped her head, lacing my fingers into her hair. "I promise. You believe me, don't you?"

"Yes."

Her voice held uncertainty, but her emotions were steady. I had no idea which to believe. Maybe neither did she. She twisted her head to stare at the seat in front of us, but I caught it and twisted it back.

"Becca..."

"It's your sole reason for existing, and you are damn good at your job, right?" she offered me a fake smile. "Of course I believe you."

"Then what..."

"Stop badgering the girl, Cael. Let her get some rest." Ethan tapped her legs in what I could only imagine was comfort before he settled into the driver's seat. He was shielding her from me, but try as I might, I couldn't figure out why. They both had closed themselves off so thoroughly I could sense nothing but determination. Neither would even look my direction for the duration of the trip back to the city.

By the time we pulled up to her house, I was in full panic mode. I walked her to the door and was doing everything I knew to try and convince her to let me stay. Not surprising, she'd have none of it.

"You have work, Cael. Whatever it is, you and Ethan handle it. Just promise to be safe."

"That's my line."

"I'm going to check on Billy's family. Take them a cell phone, batteries, bottled water. A simple errand. No Columbian drug lord missions, I swear," she joked to try and lighten my mood. "Well, they were just simple fishermen the last time I checked anyway."

I trailed a finger down her cheek, unable to hide my concern. "You'll call as soon as you get home?"

"Ethan's wearing off on you," she grumbled. "The overprotective thing-"

The comparison incensed me, and I said the first thing that popped into my head. "I've allowed you to have my dick in your mouth. I think I've earned some privileges."

"Allowed? Seriously?"

Would I ever learn the right thing to say to her? I grabbed her arms before she could flee. "You pulled me back when even Ethan couldn't, Becca. I don't want to lose that the moment I found it."

"That wasn't so hard, was it?" she murmured and stretched to offer me a warm kiss. "I'll call as soon as I'm home."

CHAPTER SEVEN

Cael

Ethan didn't even give me a chance to ask what the hell he and Becca were hiding. Instead, as soon as we arrived at the Row, he tucked Sarah in front of the television with a bottle of weak wine and then he and I went to work going through files. His phone call had all the Saints on high alert, and they'd pulled hundreds of documents for us to thread through. None of us even knew exactly what we were looking for, but we were looking nonetheless. After a few hours, I had given up and was watching Sarah's movie, but Ethan's dedication was absolute.

"Ethan, the county emergency manager is on line one for you."

He didn't even bother to look up from the ancient leather diary he was reading. "Remind him we don't do natural disasters."

"It's not about the storm. There's an issue brewing over in Algiers."

"Becca is in Algiers," Sarah said, not bothering to raise her head out of Ethan's lap.

"Of course she is," he sighed.

I couldn't help the dark chuckle that escaped. "That's where Billy's family is, hm?"

"Can you ever be serious?" he huffed. "Christ, is that girl ever *not* in trouble?"

"What the hell are you mad at me for? It's not like I bought the damn house for them."

Sarah glanced back and forth between the two of us, and I knew her amusement was going to irritate Ethan. Where safety was concerned, he took nothing lightly. Before I could warn her, she laughed. "So this is what stressed Saints look like. Fascinating."

"She's your sister," Ethan spat, getting up and striding across the room to take the call. Quick and efficient, he was back to us in minutes. "Riots and looting. Believed to be storm related. There are tactical teams on the ground, but they don't have enough men."

"We have Saints on duty over there," I offered.

"I gave him their number."

Sarah nodded and stretched back out on the sofa, her hand going for the television remote.

"Really?" Ethan sent her a reprimanding glare.

"She's been getting out of shit since she was five, Ethan. Riots in this city won't even raise her heart rate."

"Sarah-"

She sent him a kinder smile and patted the place beside her. "She is my sister, Ethan, and I love her. But if I worried every time she was in some dangerous situation I could never get out of bed. She's fine until she tells me she's not."

It didn't make him stop worrying, but it did make him sit back down beside her. By the third hour, though, when every television show was interrupted with video crews from the scene in Algiers, even Sarah's calm was beginning to wear thin. As the violence continued to escalate, the more phone calls Ethan took. We sent another dozen men to help, ones fresh and rested from being at the Row, and I finally took over the duty roster to check on every man we had in the field. I had confirmed 89 of the 140 spread throughout the city when Ethan touched my shoulder.

"She just showed up on the *Queen*."

I clicked the phone off, already rising and heading for my coat. "Who found her?"

"No one. Clint's on duty and said she just showed up at the dock. He tucked her into one of the suites. Exhausted and filthy but she refused medical care."

I hesitated with my arm halfway in my jacket. "She got there on her own?"

Sarah gave a soft laugh from her perch on the sofa. "Told you so."

I took several steps toward the door before remembering I'd been doing an assignment of my own. I turned, but Ethan waved off my words before the discussion could even begin.

"Go. If she's safe, the Saints have no excuse not to be safe as well."

"Don't use her for comparison," Sarah demanded, rising to join us. "I'll do the call list. Go get my sister, Cael."

The roads were deserted, making the trip to the riverboat quick and uneventful. Even so, it felt like hours before I stepped foot on the dock. Clint was waiting at the end but could offer no additional information about how she arrived. Instead, he just directed me to the suite he'd given her and wished me luck. I had no idea what that even meant.

My gaze traveled slow and steady over each inch of her. Stray bits of leaves, trash and whatever else she'd crawled through to escape tangled in her mess of hair. Mud and creosote streaked across her bare arms and down the length of her tanned legs. Her shorts and t-shirt were intact but coated with a thin layer of black river sediment that told me she'd waded through the river banks at least for some part of her ordeal. Smart, really. Not many people would be willing to risk the industrial sewage milkshake that was the Mississippi River just to chase one single girl. Grimy and exhausted, but she was physically unscathed. I was beginning to think the girl could walk through fire and remain unblemished. She is absolutely, perfectly, magnificent. Damn her.

I trailed a single finger up her thigh. "Hey."

Her eyes flashed open without even a flicker of fear. *Passion. Desire. Desperation.* It flooded through me like a solid presence in the room, as thick and choking as the storm soaked fog rolling in outside. Tiny fists clenched my collar, and I allowed her to pull our bodies together. Her mouth surged against mine, hard and unrelenting. My hands tangled into her hair, pulling her head back to face me. "Becca-"

"You, Cael. I came here, I waited here, for you."

Need. The one emotion I'd been waiting to sense from her and, now that it had arrived, it pierced into my soul with the force of a thousand raindrops through drought-starved air.

I pulled her off the bed, struggling to get her damp clothes stripped off. Impatient, she swatted my hand away and took them off herself. She stood in place, allowing my eyes to rake over her. Her breasts, round and firm, her nipples already stiff and begging to be licked and suckled. Her toned stomach, her hips perfect handholds for thrusting into her, and her tiny bare shaven sex, already glistening with desire. My cock twitched at the mere sight of her, knowing how tight and wet she would be. Tiny...so fucking tiny. "If I hurt you, you have to tell me."

She stepped into me, her lips going straight for my throat. "If you hurt me," she promised, "I'll likely beg for more."

God, this woman would be the death of me. I cupped her face in my hands, forcing her to look at me. "Safety first, Becca. Give me one word, so I know to stop."

She didn't even flinch. "Mercy."

"Mercy it is."

I buried my body into hers, pinning her against the wall. Before I could kiss her, her hands assaulted my chest, slender fingers popping each shirt button free. She had moved on to my pants when I finally felt it: fear buried under the passionate frenzy. My hands hovered over hers, unwilling to stop her but determined to slow her: I needed to understand.

"You're trembling. Becca-"

But she knew my own fear and brushed it away with a tender kiss in the center of my chest. "I'm not afraid of you," she promised. "But right now, I don't need questions. I need you."

My hands released her, slipping up her curves to cradle her hands in my face. My lips pressed into hers, slow but unyielding. She wriggled, trying to persuade me with her body to forego any gentleness. Her fingers braided into my hair in a futile attempt to force me harder into her. I broke my kiss only long enough to give a low chuckle. It was enough to let her know this was war: until she surrendered every emotion to desire, I wasn't going to give in. I wanted every part of her to be mine, and I refused to accept anything less.

In one fumbling move, I had my pants off and kicked my legs free. I stepped into her, delighting in the way her breath hitched as my cock pressed hard into her pixie frame. Her fingers wrapped around me, stroking my shaft in long, hard pulls. Every few strokes a finger would find its way over the tip of my cock and rub along the wetness, sending a spasm through me. I dropped my mouth to the curve of her throat, my breath hot and ragged against her skin. Now she gave a soft triumphant laugh, and I wanted to hate that she was being as obstinate and controlling as me. She was absolutely maddening...which made me want her even more.

"So sassy," I murmured.

My hand slipped to her inner thigh, trailing up and teasing her folds until a soft moan escaped. I circled around them, slow and hard, before slipping a finger inside. I gave her only a breath before thrusting in another, the heel of my hand pressing hard against her clit. A desperate moan escaped, and her head dropped back against the wall. She looked ready to collapse, and I snaked one arm around her waist at the same instant her fiery desire took hold. It was powerful enough to make me take a step back to look into her eyes...but the only reflection was my own. Thank god. I wasn't sure how much longer I could've resisted.

"Play later," she demanded, "take me now."

I grasped her shoulders, spinning her towards the bed. In a few stumbling steps, she was across the bed on all fours. I grasped my cock, threading it into her in a single long, slow stroke. I stayed still for a few breaths, memorizing the way she felt around me: warm and wet, a silky yet iron tightness that was indescribable. Her hips bucked with impatience, and I gave a hard thrust in warning. But she was never one to be submissive.

Her face tipped over her shoulder as she buried herself down on me. "For chrisssakes, Cael, stop thinking you'll break me and fuck me the way we both want you to."

I squeezed her breast hard with one hand and raked my nails down her back with the other, my cock starting a pounding, punishing rhythm inside her. My balls slapped against her ass, her head dropping against the pillows as her moans grew louder and louder. Her fingers flashed to her clit, rubbing in tiny, desperate circles. I couldn't help the possessive growl that rose in my throat. "Mine."

I twisted her hand away, replacing it with my own. My palm blanketed her sex, my thumb flicking hard and furious against her. My name flew from her throat over and over in low, guttural pleas. She came first but only by seconds, her muscles contracting viselike and pulling me along right after.

Her body dropped to the bed, hard and exhausted. It took every ounce of energy I had left not to collapse on top of her, and I rolled onto my back, sweat sliding off every inch of my skin. She was so still for so long that I almost believed she'd gone to sleep. But as her desire was satiated, a hurricane of other emotions was starting to flicker back to life. I tugged her over to rest on my chest, and her fingers began drawing invisible patterns on my skin. I didn't need to ask what they were.

"Between the mud, the sweat and the sex, I think I owe the *Crescent Queen* some new bed linens."

"I'll take care of it." I let my fingers trail up and down her bare shoulder, trying to tame the unease I could feel rising. Yet, the more tender my touches became, the more tension that etched through her muscles. For all the calm she brought out in me, I only seemed to be stressing her out more. "Becca..."

She offered me a forced smile before breaking free and shuffling off the bed.

"Christ, could it get any more humid?" She strode across the room, sliding the windows open as far as they would go. The wind whipped through the room, hot and heavy, and I knew we were back to pulling fucking teeth.

"The storm is close."

She nodded but didn't respond, intent on lifting her hair and getting some air circulating against her skin.

"Was it rough over in Algiers?"

"No. Just a bunch of drunken kids. Waiting for the storm, celebrating a day of hard labor securing their houses."

"Becca," I chastised, "the emergency manager called the Saints in for assistance."

"Yes." She flashed me an impatient glare. "When the cops showed up it turned into something entirely different."

"Ah, a self-fulfilling prophecy. They thought the crowd meant riots, but the kids only fought back when accused of rioting. New Orleans at its finest. Let me guess; you tried to be the voice of reason?"

"I forgot how dedicated both sides are to their cause," she murmured and stuck her hands out the window, catching the first droplets of rain as it began to fall.

"How did you get out?"

"I'm creative when need be."

It was barely an answer. The type of answer you'd give when distracted and thinking of something else. She was purposefully blocking me out, concentrating on each rain drop. If her face was any indication, she was counting them to keep her emotions hidden.

"What aren't you telling me? You know I'll read it in the reports when I get back to the Row."

"It was a little dicey trying to get back across after they shut down the ferries and started detaining all the boats but, really, it was nothing."

So damn frustrating. I was silent a few seconds before I couldn't stand it anymore. "Then why did you run to me?"

"I don't run to you in need of protection, Cael."

"Sadly, that's true. So why?"

She frowned, and I could sense her irritation spiking. I wasn't sure if it was directed at herself or me, but even when irritated, she was still sexy as hell. She stepped back to the bed, shaking enough to throw water droplets across my skin. Her rain chilled hands pressed into my chest, her fingernails tracing over my muscles.

"You are trying to distract me."

"It's working," she grinned, her eyes flickering down to my rising cock and then back again.

"Such confidence," I murmured. "Tell me why, Becca."

She huffed. "Because I realized you were the only place I wanted to be."

"That wasn't so hard, was it?" I chuckled and lifted her to straddle my waist. "I'm a place now? Are all the Riley women as exasperating as you or did I just get lucky?"

"You got *very* lucky," she said, giving me a devilish wink.

I pinched her nipples, hard and quick, in retaliation. "Is that true or are you just desperate to have me inside you again?"

"Both," she grinned. "Don't you know? Can't you tell?"

I hesitated, and she felt the change in me. Her eyes locked on mine, and a rush of worry flooded into the room. "Cael?"

"Stop worrying. It's not a sexy look for you. I just find your emotions very hard to discern," I admitted. "I don't trust that I'm reading the right ones."

Guilt rushed through her, and I couldn't even fathom what that meant. Before I could ask, her lips were soft on mine, her fingers gentle and exploring along the lines of my jaw. Her voice was a tiny whisper at my throat, a guilty admission that she clearly never wanted to voice: "You are becoming home."

For a woman that traveled the world, that had watched her family be torn away and her memories splintered into haunting prisms, it was the most significant thing she could have ever said. She could've said she loved me, but I wouldn't have believed her. She could've said she wanted me in bed, but I'd have known it was only a half truth. She might have said protection, but I knew she was fearless. Instead, she granted me a tiny sliver of her soul.

And I had no fucking idea how to respond. I kissed her long and deep, waiting for some eloquent response to filter into my brain, but nothing came. She didn't sigh or frown. There was no sense of frustration or expectation in her. Only longing and for that, I did have a response.

I gave her one last kiss before gripping her hips and sliding her down my body. She shifted, her body grinding down on me, and a slow, luxurious contentment washed over her. She circled her hips, causing my cock to spiral inside her as she continued to pump up and down. A new physical sensation rippled through me, growing and building as her muscles revolved around me.

"Oh...goddamn, Becca," I breathed as her moves sent wave after wave of ecstasy through my body. "Where the fuck did you learn that?"

"Singapore."

I grasped the headboard behind me for support. "I owe them a debt of gratitude. Don't stop," I growled. "Don't ever fucking stop."

Her movements rolled through me like a tide taking me to the edge and back down again, over and over. I could stay here forever like this, flush with erotic contentment and endless need for her. Her and no one else. It was the closest I'd ever come to complete fulfillment in my entire life. My eyes flickered open, watching her: her head thrown back, messy hair cascading like a chaotic waterfall down her back; her body curved in a perfect arch to take me in deeper; her palms cupping her breasts and kneading her nipples between her thumb and forefinger. I'd never been with someone so confident, so vibrant, so passionate. It was captivating.

Captivating. I could feel her pulling us under, into a world where nothing else existed. But, deep down in the recesses of her thoughts, a flicker of grief remained. It was my fault. I had brought the memories back with the mere mention of the Riley women and now when I chanced a look at her, all I could imagine was someone branding Becca like they had her mother. And if she dropped us into a world of our own, I knew...I could not protect her.

"Becca, think of something else."

But I had lost her. She was too close to the edge to hear anything. Flashes of bleeding runes emblazoned all over her body assaulted me. I squeezed my eyes shut, my breath choking in my throat.

"Becca, please, please-" I begged as I felt her orgasm come, her muscles contracting violently around my cock. "Becca, mercy!"

She was trained well, lurching off of me in a breath. The suction of her fast retreat caused an unwelcome orgasm to rip through me, painting her thigh with se-men. She moved to the opposite edge of the bed, her arms folding over her chest as stinging rejection continued to course through her.

I knew she would not come near me until I gave her permission...that was how safety worked. I gave it a full minute for both our emotions to settle before I reached a hand out to her. "Come here," I demanded, my voice still low and hoarse.

Worry washed over her, and she shuffled close, her hands cupping my face and tracing around my eyes.

"You called mercy because of your emotions?" she guessed with a forced smile. "That's such a man thing to do."

She was forgiving me. Damn it all to hell.

I wanted to tell her everything. To tell her the power she possessed, to tell her of the abilities stirring within her that she didn't even know existed. Even the half ass theories we had about her lineage. But the rules were absolute: we could not tell humans what they didn't already recognize about themselves. It could change their decisions, their paths, lives, and future. It would be an unforgivable breach of our rules.

"Will it always be like this?" she whispered. "Whatever just happened, is there a way to prevent it? A way for me not to hurt you?"

"We'll find a way, yes." I forced lightness into my voice. "We're too good in bed together to not find a way."

"Good? Did you just say good?" She frowned, but her eyes were sparkling with mischief, and I couldn't help but grin.

"Adequate? Above average?"

"Above average my ass," she huffed.

Before she could twist away, I tugged her down onto the bed, kissing her long and hard. "Phenomenal. Spectacular. Miraculous."

"Better, much much better," she laughed. "Who would've guessed the dark and brooding Cael Saint had a playful side?"

"Only with you. Now," I nuzzled her neck, "go get a shower. You're covered in mud, and you smell like me."

"I rather like the way you smell."

"Go," I nudged her. "You've got about five minutes."

"I have a time limit? Kiss my-"

"I'll kiss whatever location you demand, sweetheart, but I'm starving, and while we were in the throws of passion, the *Queen* went on generator power. So unless you want a cold shower-"

She gave me a quick kiss and hopped off the bed. "Enough said. Meet you in the galley in four minutes."

CHAPTER EIGHT

Becca

The hot water didn't last nearly long enough to clear my muddled thoughts. Through all my sexual encounters, whether a quick hookup or a short-lived but repeated liaison, I never allowed myself to utter my partner's name. It was a conscious choice. A way to keep them a faded, blurry memory. But tonight that had changed. I called Cael's name not once but a dozen times. Even before we made it to bed, when I was escaping Algiers, it was his name on repeat in my head, driving me forward.

I stepped out of the shower and tugged on a guest robe, hesitating at the mirror to see if I looked different. Of course not. I shook my head, cursing my own idiocy, before heading down to the kitchen to join him.

I peered around the giant refrigerator. "Find anything?"

"Leftovers from the party or sandwiches."

"Sandwiches."

"Excellent choice." He handed me a stack of ingredients and then grabbed a handful himself. I placed them down on the butcher block, and he nuzzled my neck as I moved aside to give him space.

"You smell like...." His nose wrinkled. "Almonds."

"That doesn't look like approval," I chuckled. "Fancy designer soap in your shower. Might want to have the staff rethink that if the smell offends you."

He set to work, building us two enormous sandwiches, tucking food in his mouth as he worked. "You just don't smell like you."

"And what's that?" I struggled to try and hop up on the counter, but they were too high for me even to come close. Without missing a breath, he reached over and lifted me onto it with one arm before returning to his work.

"A winter's night."

"What?"

He popped a cucumber slice in his mouth and shrugged. "You know, when you walk outside in winter. Crisp, clean air that has this anticipation of snow and a hint of old fashioned log fires."

"Poetic," I grinned.

"Fact not poetry."

"Ironic really considering how little snow, much less real winters that I've encountered in my life. Are you going to share any of that food or just keep nibbling until there's nothing left for me?"

He whirled, presenting me a plate with a sandwich almost as big as my head. I laughed as I accepted it. "Saint size, I take it?"

He gave me a salacious grin. "You weren't complaining about that earlier."

I wasn't even going to touch that one and picked off some of the sandwich toppings to eat. "You smell like sunshine. Even at midnight. I figured it was a Saint thing."

He continued to gobble his sandwich, and I offered him one of the hot beers sitting on the counter. He nodded his thanks. "Does Ethan smell like that?"

I frowned, thinking. "No. Just regular cologne, I guess. Does that mean something?"

He shrugged. "Not to me but, as I said, I'm not a scholar. Just a curiosity perhaps."

Uncertainty flooded through me, and his eyes darted my direction. "Do you believe that?"

"No, I suppose I don't," he admitted but then winked. "I don't believe our sense of smell indicates any dark forces at work either so stop worrying."

I put down my food, kicking my legs in impatience. He was watching me, evaluating my emotions but, for once, I didn't care. I blew out a frustrated sigh. "Cael, what are we going to do?"

"You don't seem the planning type."

"I'm not, but you Saints are."

"True, very true."

He pushed our plates aside and moved to stand in front of me. His hands dragged up my thighs, pushing the robe away.

"I intend on waiting out the storm right here with you," he murmured as he worked to untie the belt and expose all of me. "Where I will take my time kissing, licking, and tasting every stunning inch of you." His lips tucked into my throat, his tongue sliding against my flesh. His mouth slid lower, taking my breast in his mouth. He took long, slow sucks of my nipple and my hands flew to his head. He gave me a wicked grin and moved to suckle the other, his teeth nibbling against me.

"You are a tease," I grumbled.

"A tease? Did you just call me a tease?" He laughed then spread my legs wider, his mouth burying hard into my sex. It was so fast, so unexpected that I bolted upward. His arm wrenched around me, locking me in place. "You taste unfucking believable."

His tongue was rough against my folds, flicking hard against my clit. He pulled me tighter against his face, his tongue darting inside me.

"Christ, Cael..."

My juices coated him; his tongue now slick against me. He moved back to my clit, circling and sucking at a furious pace. My hips arched toward him as a desperate plea rose in my throat...and then he was gone. He jerked away, yanking my robe over me, and then whirled to stand in front of me at the same moment a shadow appeared in my periphery.

"Now that is my kind of meal. Willing to share, brother?"

"Slithering out of the fog, Micah? I see your penchant for dramatic immaturity hasn't changed."

Ignoring Cael, he turned in my direction. "You must be Becca Riley. I daresay I have many more years of experience than young Cael here. Why don't you allow me-"

I was still coming down from the interruption, still breathless and trying to process what had just happened. My eyes darted to the man who had joined us: tall, dark, arrogant and impeccably well dressed. A Saint, yes, but not one with the common decency or propriety that Ethan required of his men. "You," I hissed, "are a perverted asshole that needs to go away."

A soft chuckle filtered through the darkness as another man, older but otherwise identical, strode forward. "My apologies. He doesn't get out very often. It affects his manners."

"Gabriel." Cael's voice was steady, but I could feel his muscles turn to stone.

Both men jerked their heads toward Micah, who was still leering at me with a smug grin. I didn't need any special powers to know what dirty thoughts were going through his mind.

"Micah, go tour the Quarter."

"There's a fucking hurricane-"

Gabriel's eyes flashed, and he whirled on him. He didn't like being questioned. "Don't be dramatic. It's a tropical storm. Maybe the rain will wash away the mud soiling your filthy fucking brain."

As soon as he was gone, Cael's body relaxed. Still on alert, still tense, but not ready to kill everyone. "Does Ethan know you've arrived?"

He nodded. "I had your man down at the dock call him. I've asked him to join us as soon as the storm abates."

"He doesn't give a damn about the rain. He'll be here shortly."

"I figured as much. Introduce me to the lady you're hiding, Cael. A proper introduction."

Cael helped me down from the table, his hand resting on my neck to keep me close. "Becca Riley, meet Gabriel Saint. He is based in Florence and is one of those scholars I keep mentioning. Research, history, imparting his worldly knowledge on us lesser beings, that kind of thing."

I glanced from one to the other, wishing I had some indication if he was friend or foe. I thought the Saints were inseparable, all for one and the rest of that Musketeer bullshit. Clearly, there was some internal politics at work I didn't yet understand.

"A wizened old sage?" I asked.

"Old is relative but, yes, something like that. We each have our talents, you know."

"No, I don't."

"Ethan's is leadership. People will walk through fire for him. And Cael's...well, I'm beginning to get my own opinions about where his talent lies." He sent a thoughtful glance Cael's direction before turning back to me. "Our specialties evolve over time, our talents getting honed as the years progress. Much like your photography skills, I imagine. Come, let's sit."

He motioned toward the dining room. Cael hesitated before nodding. Threading our fingers together, he followed Gabriel to a table.

"I do apologize for interrupting. The fog puts our senses off. I would never have-"

"We get it. You're a gentleman."

I shivered at the anger in Cael's voice, but Gabriel gave me a dismissive wave. "No worries. I'd be hostile about such an untimely interruption as well."

"Why are you here, Gabe?"

"An etching placed outside the Row? Surely you didn't think that would go unnoticed."

"Perhaps we should wait on Ethan."

"I really can't afford to do that," Gabe sent us both an apologetic look before leaning towards me. "I had the privilege of seeing one of your exhibitions in Prague, eighteen months ago. It was stunning...it took my breath away actually. You are extraordinarily talented, Becca."

"Coming from him, that may be more a threat than a compliment," Cael muttered.

It was a warning for me but not one I could decipher. I bit my lower lip as Cael's tension begin to infect me.

"Relax, brother, you misunderstand," Gabe murmured. "I'm here on an official mission to check on the etching outside the Row. My concern for you and Becca, however, is a personal and private matter."

"That's certainly something I wouldn't want to miss." Ethan's voice caused all of us to turn. "Fog and storms are a bitch to the senses, aren't they? People just sneak up on you. Damned unnerving, isn't it? Almost like being human again."

I knew the snarky, drinking, lovesick Ethan but this was someone completely different. He strode in, taking control with just his presence. He wasn't physically bigger, but it was as if his entire being filled the room, leaving space for nothing and no one else. He stopped at my chair, resting his hand on my head until I looked up at him. "You alright?"

"I didn't mean to scare her, Ethan. That's not my intent."

"Gabe, I've only known one thing to scare her and it sure as hell isn't you." He leaned down, kissing my cheek, hovering at my ear. "She's safe at the Row."

For once, I was glad how well they knew me. I nodded, even managing a brief smile. "I'm fine."

"Go sit in Cael's lap, would you? He'll let you know if there's something you shouldn't answer."

"Ethan, you're being ridiculous-"

"My town, my rules."

Cael

Ethan's appearance changed everything. New Orleans *is* his town, and Gabriel had no authority here. Ethan could order him to leave if he wanted and I knew, if he got out of line with Becca, Ethan wouldn't hesitate.

I took her hand, pulling her into my lap. Now that she knew Sarah was safe, her normal curiosity and calm echoed through us. I smiled then turned her wrist to trace along it and was greeted with a brief wiggle of her eyebrows which made me chuckle.

"Their emotions-" Gabriel murmured.

"Like a fucking hurricane, I know." Ethan moved to us, kneeling in front of Becca and tucking something in her hand. He wrapped her fingers around it, creating a fist to keep it hidden. Then he tucked her arm into her lap with a light thump. His voice dropped to a bare whisper. "Right here, nowhere else. Okay?"

Bless her, she didn't even hesitate and followed his order instantly, locking whatever he'd given her against her thigh. Despite her intense curiosity, she didn't even chance a look into her palm. I guess one way she stayed alive through all those wars, all those days behind enemy lines, had been by never second guessing the rules she was given. Fucking incredible. How could you not love a girl like that?

As soon as the thought hit me, my eyes shot to Ethan and Gabriel. But they hadn't caught my emotion which meant whatever he'd tucked in her hand was rune etched. Ethan had built us a wall of protection. Suddenly, I loved him too. What the fuck was this woman doing to me?

"Well, that should settle some things," Ethan said, sinking into a chair next to Gabriel. "So what brings you to my lovely city in the middle of a raging storm?"

"The rune outside-"

"I have the authority to place a rune wherever the hell I please."

"That doesn't stop the Council from being curious. Just tell me it was necessary, and we can move on."

"It was necessary," I spat before I could contain it.

Ethan smiled. "I don't think I need defending, Cael, but I appreciate it."

"No, you absolutely do not. See? Walk through fire for him," Gabe gave Becca a brief smile before turning to me. "Your blind loyalty to the Saints seems to have diminished. Do I have Ethan to thank for that or are you just growing up?"

Becca shifted in my lap, and I could feel her defenses rising. "Do I need to be here for this testosterone battle of wills or can I be excused?"

"He's here for you, Becca. The rune is just an excuse so if you don't mind-"

My eyes flashed to Ethan's, but he held a hand up to keep me calm. Or ordering me to at least *act* calm. I let out a low hiss. "Get on with it then, Gabe."

He nodded and pulled a crumpled photo out of his breast pocket. "I know you take thousands of photos, and it's unlikely you remember even half of them, but..."

"I remember them all," she cut in, the irritation still plain in her voice. "Every single one."

She reached for the photo and, as soon as she had it, I tugged her back tight against my chest. It was a happy photograph: a boy and his mother sitting on the porch steps of a farmhouse. It was non-descript and nothing like the hard, edgy work she had on exhibit. But it caused her to tense which made me feel uneasy as well.

"This was stolen from the exhibit in Prague."

Gabe nodded. "Guilty. I can pay you for it now if you wish."

"I never take fees for my exhibits," she mumbled, her eyes still on the image.

"Really?" Ethan raised an eyebrow.

"I have no fee. If a gallery charges an admission, 85% has to go to charity, the rest to overhead. No profit. And yes, I check."

"So how do you make a living?"

"Aren't you the nosy one?" she chuckled, sending Ethan a chastising frown. "I go where others won't. News photography isn't glamorous, but the hazard pay is lucrative. I also have collectors willing to pay ridiculous sums for a single photo. Usually not even my best work but I guess eye of the beholder and all."

"Understandable," Gabe said. "I'm happy to pay whatever price you name for this one."

Ethan straightened in his seat. "Do you have a list of these collectors?"

"Of course."

"Can you-"

"Your price for this one?" Gabe interrupted.

Urgent. Desperate. I could hear it in his voice. And so could Becca.

She hesitated and her head turned just slightly Ethan's direction. Whatever non-verbal discussion they had, she turned back to Gabe and shook her head. "I don't need your money. Tell me why you want it so badly, and it's yours."

Ethan smiled. It was exactly what he wanted her to say.

"And my questions?"

"I have nothing to hide," she spat at the same moment I squeezed her hand to keep her silent.

She had plenty to hide where her photography was concerned...she just didn't realize it. "She's losing patience," I interrupted, to cover my unease. "And so am I, Gabe."

"You can choose not to believe me, but I am risking my life, my soul, my position by talking to you all. I've waited, I've been patient, and when the etching outside the Row gave me an excuse, I used it. Believe me or not, it's the truth. I am not here to cause harm to any of you or your city. It's a very personal and private mission; I swear to you."

The problem with erecting a wall for Becca and me was that it blocked the men from me as well: I had no way to know if he was telling the truth.

"I believe you," Ethan murmured. "Becca, if you can, will you help him please?"

Help. Not just answer him but help. Gabriel Saint, the defender of all relics and the preeminent Council historian, needed help. Becca's eyes turned to me, waiting for my decision. I'd forgotten that she didn't need to follow Ethan. "Despite the geography, he is my brother as well. Please."

She nodded. "What do you want to know?"

Heartbreak etched across Gabe's face, and he leaned closer. "Where was this taken? Why were you there? What made you choose them? Did you talk to them, know them? Anything?"

Becca studied the photo, and I could feel her confusion taking hold. I squeezed her wrist. "If you don't know-"

"I do," she cut me off. "He just isn't the first person to ask about this photo and that rarely happens." She handed the photo back to him. "It was taken in Lidice, outside Prague. I was covering the flooding and Lidice made a good news story because of its history of being destroyed at the hands of Hitler. One of the bigger news outlets sent me. I spent three days at their farmhouse. Her name is Anna, and that's her son, Pavel."

"Yes," Gabe's voice broke, "that's true."

Ethan's eyes rocketed toward him. "He's your son."

Gabe nodded and the tears he was trying to contain told me the rest before he even said the words. "From before."

"Gabriel-"

"Do what you will, Ethan! I have to know!"

"Gabe," Ethan's hand was firm on his shoulder, calming him. "You are safe here. I promise. My city, my rules, remember? You are safe."

"You aren't allowed contact with your life before joining the Saints," Becca guessed. "And they are your life before."

"Yes." Gabriel straightened, his eyes imploring. "Or they were. They were killed a few months ago."

My eyes narrowed at him. "How? By who?"

"I don't know," his said, choking a little. "It's hard for me to try and get answers without raising questions."

"Becca," Ethan interrupted, "you said that someone else asked you about this particular photo?"

"The email was forwarded from the gallery in Prague. It will still be in my files." She turned a softer gaze to Gabriel, compassion filling her. "Along with the other photos of them. I took several hundred during my stay. If you want them-"

"Yes, yes, please."

Gabe's hand reached out to touch Becca in unthinking gratitude, but Ethan swatted it away. It was a clear message to Gabe but one for me as well: Ethan trusted him...but only so far.

"Ethan, if you'll run him by the loft-"

"I'll take care of it," he assured her.

Gabe's heartbroken gaze leveled on Becca. "They are happy. This photo tells me they are happy. Do your photos lie? Is the emotion theirs or yours? I just want to know that, however briefly it may have lasted, they found happiness."

Confusion poured over Becca, and she shook her head. "I don't understand."

"Please-" Gabe begged.

"She doesn't know," Ethan cut in.

"What do you mean? She has to realize." He shook his head. "It's the most extraordinary-"

"She doesn't know," Ethan's voice was a dangerous growl, cutting off whatever Gabriel was going to say.

Gabriel dropped back in his seat, his eyes flickering between all of us. "Your town, your rules," he acquiesced in complete defeat.

Unfortunately, Becca would never be defeated. "Ethan."

"Now isn't-"

"Ethan." Her voice was quiet, solemn and I could feel the conflict coursing through her. "You warned me once, in this very room and now I'm going to give you the same courtesy. If you lie to me now, it is something we *cannot* go back from. Don't make a mistake you'll regret."

I was thankful the rune kept Ethan's emotions blocked from me. Whatever they were, they were taking a physical toll on Gabe. His body had nearly convulsed from the onslaught, his head dropping to rest in his hands. It took several minutes for Ethan to settle and he touched Gabriel light on the shoulder.

"Sorry, brother," he whispered.

Gabe nodded but clearly didn't trust his voice yet. He took in a deep, shuddering breath then straightened, his eyes leveling on Becca. "I apologize, Becca. I did come with no intention of harm."

Past tense. Which meant he intended on harming her now. I was ready to launch myself at him, and Becca's fury at Ethan was growing by the second. My adrenaline and her anger twisted together, causing both of us to turn to stone. But Ethan held up his hand, his voice a normal, calming cadence.

"Both of you, relax and stop jumping to the worst of conclusions. I just need a breath. Allow me that."

I turned her free arm over in my lap, tracing the veins with slow, methodical precision. It was as much to comfort myself as it was to ease her tension. "You know Saints can feel the emotions of others. Sense it, breath it in."

"Yes."

"It doesn't transfer," Gabe offered. "I mean, if you are sad, it doesn't mean Cael is sad."

Ethan gave a halfhearted chuckle. "Bad example."

"I get it," Becca said, her voice still icy. "People's emotions don't influence your own emotions."

"As you'd expect, things don't give off emotions. Physical items. The chair you are sitting in, the tablecloth, whatever."

She nodded at Gabe. "That's heartening. I'd hate to imagine a chair's emotion when someone sits their big ass down on it." Her sarcasm has its intended effect, and everyone gave soft grins. "Please, Ethan-"

"In your photos, you capture emotion. Emotion we can sense as if it is our own."

"I don't-"

Gabe waved the photo of Anna and her son. "This one? They are happy. It's not their smiles or their demeanor. I can feel their happiness just as if it is my own. I look at it and feel goodness in the world, a future."

"Same," Ethan nodded.

Becca's eyes drifted to mine in question, and I nodded. "Yes, it's the same for me."

"And if you see a dying child in the street, everyone gets sad. I really don't understand the difference."

Ethan glanced to Gabe for help, to find some way to make her understand.

"Becca, we rely on emotional discernment to do our job. Our entire way of being, our lives, are based on it. For someone to be able to influence them, to make us feel what they desire instead of the truth, the consequences can be devastating."

"If you can make me feel a person has murderous tendencies, they would be killed," Ethan provided. "If you make me feel all hope is lost, I'd be suicidal. If you make me feel a person is untrustworthy and I believe that is my own emotion, my own discernment, then I would never ally with them again."

"It could destroy nations much less individual men."

Her eyes locked with mine, something dark and unreadable settling inside her. My eyes darted to Ethan, trying to warn him to tread carefully. Wherever her thoughts were taking her, it was nowhere good.

"How?" she asked, her attention back on them. "How is that possible?"

"We don't know yet. We've never come across anything like this before."

I opened my mouth and closed it again. I *did* understand how she accomplished it but now wasn't really the appropriate time to explain how I'd come by that knowledge.

"Cael?" Ethan's voice was tight, worried.

"Nothing," I murmured. "Later."

She didn't even acknowledge me. "And Saints?"

"What do you mean?"

"Cael said it could destroy nations and regular men. What about Saints?"

Gabe spoke before either Ethan or I could stop him. "Uncontrollable. No, uncontainable. We succeed in our duties through our ability to contain and compartmentalize our emotions. For someone to have power over that? To be able to prevent us from silencing things and discerning what is truth and what is fictional? It would tear into our very souls."

Ethan didn't even need to meet my gaze to know Becca was retreating. Her body language made it obvious to everyone in the room. He tried to smile, but the effect was less than reassuring. "That's a scholar's conjecture, of course. We don't understand it well enough to know-"

"No, it's not just conjecture," she whispered.

She shifted in my lap, ignoring Ethan's order about the rune. I could see the men flinch as her emotions hit them full force. Like going from midnight to noon in the span of a breath, both men were blinded by the instantaneous assault. They dropped their heads to their knees, struggling to regain their composure. But Becca was oblivious, her eyes only on me. "Earlier," she whispered, "mercy?"

I nodded, unable to vocalize my personal thoughts. Ethan and Gabe were getting themselves back under control, but that meant their conflicted emotions were now ravaging through me. There were only three Saints and yet we were destroying each other. I was still trying to sort through them when Becca's emotions streamed through me with prismatic clarity.

Need. Longing. Love. Acceptance. Sacrifice. They all washed through her in the span of a breath, leaving only cool resignation in their wake. She stroked my cheek, resting her palm against it as her lips moved in a long, slow dance against mine. "Stay safe, Cael. Watch over Sarah."

This was what she had been hiding, what had scared her beyond reason, what Ethan had sensed but I could not: desperation. For a home. For a Saint. For me.

She was gone before my thoughts, much less my voice, had time to catch up.

"Sacrificing her wants and needs for a Saint of all things," Gabe murmured. "What an extraordinary little human."

"Fuck you." I launched from my seat, but Ethan's arm blocked me.

"Let her go, Cael."

"You can't order me-"

"I'm not ordering you. I'm telling as your brother that she needs space and she won't appreciate you invading her most private of emotions right now." He tightened his grip on my shoulder. "I have more confidence in you than you have in yourself. You are worth fighting for, brother, and she'll see that soon enough."

CHAPTER NINE

Cael

The "war" room at the Row wasn't very well named. No wall of security cameras or whiteboards to plan strategy. It wasn't even big enough to hold all of us at once. Instead, a dozen of the men were sitting around an oak dining table while others stood behind. The majority were lining the nearest hallway. Ethan was pacing at the head of the table, his fury probably strong enough to reach the guards on gate duty outside. I sat to the right of his empty chair, surprisingly calm.

"You are the best contingent in the world. I'd stake my life on it. So will someone please tell me how the fuck you can't find a single, helpless little girl?"

"We've been shadowing her for months, Ethan. She's neither helpless or little, and you damn well know it."

"That's the answer you want to stick with?" he growled. "That's a fucking excuse."

"Stop taking it out on them because you're pissed at yourself," I murmured. "Waste as many resources as you want, but it won't change anything. Becca Riley won't be found until she wants to be found."

"It's been two days," one of the newer men was idiot enough to interrupt. "Is she even still in the city?"

"I don't-"

"Yes," I cut him off. "She wouldn't leave her sister alone this week."

"Sarah hasn't seen her."

"Irrelevant. Becca would not leave her."

"Your calm is more irritating than all of their ineptitude." He gave a sweeping arm movement over the men, causing a mixture of confusion and indignation to cloak the room.

I stood, squaring off with him. "That," I hissed, "you will apologize for."

Ethan's face stayed on mine only seconds before drifting over the broken faces of his men. He nodded. "I'm sorry. You all know that I am. I'm just-"

"Scared for her. We all know that as well so there's no point in trying to be manly about it." I turned to the men, offering them a shrug. "Somebody find us a bottle of whiskey and just keep doing what you're doing."

They nodded, each touching Ethan's shoulder as they left the room: a signal of forgiveness, camaraderie, a promise to their leader. Once they were gone and the whiskey arrived, I motioned for him to sit and poured us each a glass.

"You love her."

He didn't bother to deny it, just took a long drink. "Not like you do."

I chuckled. "Let's hope not."

He gave me a tiny smirk. "You aren't worried. Sarah's not worried."

"I didn't say I wasn't worried," I corrected. "I'm not worried about Becca keeping herself safe. I'm worried about renegade Saints finding her before we do."

"They will, you know," he murmured into his glass. "She knows to steer clear of our men. But the ones that threaten her? They are strangers she'd never think to hide from."

"I try not to think about that and hope she's chosen to hide from everyone."

"Sarah hasn't heard from her."

"You certain she's not-"

"Protecting her sister? I considered that. I have men tailing her and her phones tapped. The house, her cell, the store...all of them."

I laughed. "You better hope to hell she never finds out. Bugging your girlfriend? I'm pretty sure that's one of those lines you aren't supposed to cross."

He shrugged. "When you disappeared, I bugged every Saint at the Row. I'm willing to sink down several levels of hell for those I care about."

"Your commitment is…well, no, it's not admirable. It's invasive and shitty, truth be told. But understandable."

"Cael?"

"Hm?"

"Just shut up and drink, will you?"

It took us a good hour of complete silence to finish off the bottle. We were both dozing in our chairs when it hit us: complete, irrepressible panic. Our eyes flashed together then scanned the room for the source. Nothing. We launched out of our seats, rushing down the hall. A dozen men blocked the door, panic surging through all of them.

"Saints don't panic," Ethan hissed, low enough only for my ears. To the others, he raised his voice. "What's going on?"

"She's been found."

"Where?"

"Here. At the gate."

Rather than relief, both Ethan and I tensed. Something was crazy wrong. The men should be happy over their success, relieved their assignment was now over. Instead, it felt like they were preparing for war.

We fought our way past them and headed to the gate, but the sight caused us both to hesitate. There was an army of men blocking the gate. It stretched so deep we couldn't even see the bars. The men were all in varying states of disarray: confusion, uncertainty, curiosity. It made no sense.

"Move." Ethan's voice was commanding, but it still took several seconds for the men to clear a path.

Sarah was screaming, throwing out curse words I was surprised she even knew. I guess here was some of the Riley fire in her after all. Drying blood stained her shirt, but Becca's was still fresh, still flowing if the spreading on her shirt was any indication. Sarah kept motioning back to Becca who was growing weaker by the second. I couldn't understand a damn thing she was screaming, but when Ethan gave out a low, threatening hiss, my heart wrenched.

I could tell Becca was exhausted, could see the physical pain written across her face but where her emotions should be there was nothing. An empty blackness that enrobed every inch of her. It wasn't compassion; it wasn't grief, or fear or hurt...it was just *nothing*. No wonder the men had been thrown into a panic.

"Sarah, you're making a scene," Becca choked, her every syllable tainted with agony.

"Do I look like I give a shit?"

"You are endangering them. You're endangering Ethan."

Her eyes were still flashing, but the screaming quieted and was fast replaced with tears.

"Sarah, I know you're scared," Ethan tried. "I know you're furious-"

I grimaced. Everyone's emotions were spiraling out of control. Furious was such a gross understatement of Sarah's emotions it was almost laughable. I could feel confusion radiating from the Saints but, even more prevalent, their guilt. They didn't know *how* they had failed in their duties, but every single one knew that something had gone horribly wrong on their watch. Even Ethan was suspended somewhere between wanting to pull Sarah into his arms for comfort and wanting to send her away to protect the men.

"Becca," I cut through the chatter, my eyes leveling on her. "I need you to tell me what's happened."

"I was wrong," she managed, "I should have expected."

She thought I would understand, but there was too much swirling for me to comprehend anything. Before I could ask for clarification, Sarah broke in again.

"Who could have ever expected this?" she spat, yanking Becca toward the gates and wrenching her shirt up to reveal her stomach. "I've seen them! All over your precious Saint's Row! Our lives were normal. Normal! And then you...you fucking Saints-"

Everything else was just white noise as I focused on Becca. Her abdomen was littered with red lashes, bloodied drawings of runes that were identical to the ones that had been placed on her mother. Less intense, less deadly but still identical. Becca wouldn't meet my gaze, tight fists clenching her shirt and trying to tug it back down.

"Open the gates," Ethan barked, "get them inside. Now."

The men didn't hesitate. It was open in seconds, and they encircled both the women like bodyguards. Sarah's fists were plowing into the first one she could reach. He didn't even blink at her attempts but looked to me for direction.

"Sedate her," I ordered. "And recall Gabriel from wherever he is. We need him here now."

As soon as she was gone and the quiet settled, I turned to where Ethan was staring at Becca as if she was a puzzle he could decipher if given enough time. The gates were open, but she stood just outside, unmoving.

Her expression was unreadable, and the lack of emotions gave me nothing to go on. We didn't actually need her permission: either of us could have hauled her in with a single hand but neither of us wanted to handle it that way, and we stepped toward her in unison. Old-fashioned human way it is.

"Becca-" But she ignored me, her eyes locking on Ethan.

"Sarah's inside. Don't you want to be with her?" he tried as if she was a child. That, I knew, she wouldn't appreciate.

Her eyes narrowed. "Are you safe?"

"What?"

"Are you...all of you...the Saints...are you safe if I walk through those gates?"

Ethan opened his mouth to respond and then closed it.

"You don't know," she choked and began backing away.

Ethan's hands flashed out, digging into her shoulders and pinning her in place. "You're right, Becca, I don't know. I do know that you have no intention of harming any of them. Even ready to pass out, you are trying to protect them. Come in, let us help you, and then we'll figure it out together, okay?"

He was my boss, our leader, the brother that would sacrifice any *one* to save us all and he'd finally made his decision. I had to allow him that respect but, now that the permission was given, I had no more patience. Taking one long stride toward them, I broke his hold and scooped her into my arms.

I tucked her into my bed, moving aside to let the men try and help her. We had several former doctors and military medics in our crew, but none had the skills necessary to actually help her. Instead, they stripped her down to her underclothes, cleaned the wounds and then tried to force painkillers on her. When she launched herself at them, I had to intervene and convince her to down whiskey. It wasn't strong enough to knock her out, but at least it got her calm.

"How's Sarah?" I asked as Ethan stepped into the room.

"Still sedated. Becca?"

"You know how she is," I hissed. She was dying, slowly being bleed to death in front of us and there wasn't a damn thing we could do about it.

"How much longer would you have waited?"

"At the rate, she was losing blood? You had about eleven seconds. Where's Gabriel?"

He didn't answer, and I stiffened. "The longer it takes him to show-"

"The less you trust him. I know, and I don't disagree."

"Him being here in the city, his timing is-"

"Either a blessing or the cause. Yeah, I know that, too, Cael."

CHAPTER TEN

Cael

I had no idea how much time had passed. It was all running together where every minute moved too fast, not leaving us enough time to save her. Then she would scream, and it felt like an eternity would pass, her pain never-ending. I had folded myself into a chair, far enough away to give the medics space but close enough I could still see her every inhalation. I didn't bother to lift my gaze when the door clicked open.

Ethan dropped to kneel at my feet, his hand touching my knee. "Sarah woke a little while ago. She found Becca at the cemetery. Their mother was buried a year ago today, and she took a chance. When she arrived, she found Becca alone, bleeding in the grass, beside the tomb. Becca gave no explanation."

"She wouldn't. Not to Sarah. Not without you or I telling her it was okay."

"They left her alone," he whispered, "what kind of monster-"

Anger, guilt, and grief surged through me, whirling together in a deafening storm. "You still want to doubt who did this? Really? Does your loyalty to the Saints really stretch that fucking deep?"

"Of course not, but-" he trailed off, straightening. "You," he hissed, pivoting on his heel, "stop analyzing him. You have work to do."

My eyes shot to the door. Gabriel was hovering at the entrance, bracing himself along the door frame as my emotions continued to assault him. I narrowed my eyes, daring him to question Ethan or me. Instead, he straightened and took a steadying breath.

"Tell me what you need."

Ethan waved the medic out and shut the door. Gabe shifted deeper in the room and into Becca's field of vision. Her sharp intake of breath stirred us all to attention. Her eyes were glued to him, tension etching over her body and causing the runes to bleed again. She was growing weaker by the second, but her eyes glimmered.

"Becca," Ethan rushed toward her, touching her head, in a soothing gesture. "Stop feeling, for chrissakes. You're making it worse."

"Stop *feeling?*" she gave a strangling gasp. "Seriously?"

"You know what I mean."

But she didn't. She had no idea what he was talking about.

"Your emotions are fueling them," I explained.

"I don't understand," Gabe's confused voice moved closer. Confused and curious. Which didn't make me feel very reassured.

"She's been runemarked," Ethan murmured.

Gabe stopped mid-step. "Pardon?" His eyes landed on Becca, the runes weeping blood into a pool around her. I could see him surveying each inch of her skin, evaluating each wound. "Humans can't stop feeling. It would..."

"Kill me," Becca whispered.

"Yes, but it would be torturous. No one would ever..."

"They did," I hissed. "And this isn't the first time."

I could feel Becca's consciousness wavering, and she tried to focus her gaze on Ethan. "Sarah?"

"Here. Safe."

"Make me believe you."

"She doesn't trust the Saints?" Gabe asked.

"Would you?" Ethan spat. "She is sedated in my bed, Becca. There is no safer room in the city. Only Cael and I have access."

Her eyes drifted to Gabe. "Was this you?"

"No. God, no!" Gabe was at her side, grasping her hand. "You helped me. You gave me something no one else in the world could. Why would you ever think that?"

"Your man, your shadow-"

I didn't even try to bury the instant fury that flooded through me. "Micah."

"He's an ass, yes, but he wouldn't-"

"He didn't touch me, but he was there. He was standing beside my mother's grave when they grabbed me from behind."

"You're certain?"

Her eyes narrowed, and I knew she wasn't even going to dignify him with an answer. It didn't matter. I could feel his hatred and betrayal raging: he believed her.

He kissed the top of her head before straightening. "I'll find him."

"No." Ethan grabbed his arm before he could rush off. "I'll see to it. If he's still in the city, my men will find him."

"You don't trust me? Ethan, I swear to you-"

"I need you here, Gabe. The marks killed her mother, and now they're killing her. I have no idea how to heal them. Help her, and you'll have my trust."

He could turn Ethan down. Yes, he'd taken the same oath to protect humans that we all had...but he'd also taken the same vow to protect the Saints from potential harm as well. We had no right to ask him to get involved in such an ill-defined gray area.

But he didn't even hesitate. "I'll need some herbs, some ingredients-"

"Make a list. No modern American substitutions. There's nothing we can't find in this town."

Gabe nodded and stepped to the desk and began writing. Ethan turned my direction. "Do not leave her side. You will not go after Micah. That's an order."

"I didn't intend to."

"That's-"

"Unreasonable," Becca coughed. "Protect yourselves. Don't be idiots."

"And don't be difficult," Ethan shot back. "I don't have time for sparring with you right now."

She tried to smile, but it came out as a pain filled convulsion. "Sorry your mental capabilities are so delicate."

"Fuck you, Becca," he grumbled. He turned back to her, his hand caressing her cheek. "I'm going to have him sedate you."

"No-"

"Whatever he's going to do, it's going to hurt like hell."

"You have nine runes etched on you," Gabe explained as he handed the list to Ethan. "Think of them like magical tattoos. It's a hell of a lot easier to get a tattoo than remove one. I'm going to remove the runes the best I can. It's going to feel like I'm burning them out of your flesh, although it's more like ripping them from your soul."

"Lovely."

"You will scream-"

"Just stop. That's not necessary," I interrupted. "She's fearless but not insane. Besides, she doesn't want to scare Sarah with her screams. Sedate her and get it done."

She mouthed a 'thank you' to me at the same moment Gabe threaded a needle into her arm. I nodded but couldn't bring myself to give her a smile. Instead, I sank to sit on the edge of the bed, taking her hand in mine. "Mercy?"

"Mercy," she affirmed, her eyes already drifting closed.

As soon as she was out, Ethan's hand was on my shoulder.

"I'm not going to demand you leave but, Cael, you've got to get yourself under control. Between the guilt and the heartbreak, you are ripping Gabe and me apart. Reign it in, brother, so that we can help her."

"I can't."

"You're wrong. Anyone else wouldn't have a chance but you can and you will. For her."

Somehow he was right. I wanted to be at her side more than I wanted revenge. There would be time enough for that once she was healed. I held onto that, basking in the combination of sweet revenge and the promise of her safety. Deluded or not, it kept me calm enough that Ethan didn't have to cast me out.

Gabe tried to keep her sedated, but it didn't always work. He had to chant over the runes, three hours on each, and invariably, the sedation would wear off before he could finish. Her screams tore through the house, breaking the heart of every Saint at the Row. Ethan had to have Sarah moved to one of the outer guest houses on the property just to keep her sane. I knew why Ethan and I stayed: we both loved her. Why and how Gabe was able to stay, hour after agonizing hour, was beyond my understanding. Guilt over Micah's involvement perhaps, fear of Ethan's wrath maybe...his emotions were so intent on Becca that he allowed nothing else through.

Thirty-nine hours after he'd begun, Gabe tucked the sheet up around her, gave her a kiss on the forehead and then nodded our direction. "For now, it's what I can do. Call me when she wakes."

Ethan had two men escort him to a room to get sleep. They stood guard outside his newly assigned bedchamber: both to keep him from disappearing and to make sure no one disturbed him. Trust, it seemed, was still elusive.

When Becca finally glimmered to life, Ethan and I were at her side before her eyes managed to open completely. I helped her sit up as Ethan steadied a bottle of water to her lips. She gulped it down before waving it away. "How bad is it?"

"Gabe worked-"

"Not me. The city."

Oh. The storm. To her, it was minutes ago. To us, it was a lifetime.

"Some roofs blown off, minor flooding." Ethan shrugged. "No fatalities. I've sent most of the men out to help with storm recovery."

She nodded toward me. "If he needs to-"

"No. He doesn't." Ethan answered a little too quickly. "Billy's place is halfway underwater."

"It usually is. The locals will take care of him."

"I can send-"

"He'll just turn them away," she smiled. "His family in Algiers?"

"They are completely underwater over there. We evacuated his family to the *Crescent Queen*. We have to move it for storm cleanup so we'll just ferry them down to his place."

"Thank you, Ethan. Truly."

"Just doing our job so don't get all soft on me now."

"And Sarah?" I asked the question I knew they were both avoiding.

Ethan's hesitation caused Becca to try and struggle up, but I held her in place with one hand.

"Bourbon for breakfast, whiskey for lunch. She won't eat or even get out of bed. And her emotions..." Ethan's voice cracked. "Becca, they turn so dark, it's almost-"

"Suicidal," she murmured. She reached her hand out to take his. "Tell her I said to remember Hamar, get a shower and get her ass to work. Or Billy's to help if you think that's safer."

"But-"

"You haven't told her you love her." It was a statement with no judgment, but it cut into Ethan all the same. "She's not drowning out what happened. Her greatest fear isn't losing me; it's being alone. You only need assure her that she's not."

Ethan hovered at her forehead, offering her the lightest of kisses. "Thank you." He straightened and headed for the door. "Cael, I'll give you two a few, but don't wait too long to summon Gabe, understood?"

I waved him off in promise, my eyes never leaving Becca's. "Hamar? That's Mogadishu, right? Somalia?"

She nodded. "Gunmen stormed a hotel where I was staying. I got pretty torn up by shrapnel and other debris. The state department flew Sarah over as my next of kin."

"She must've been terrified."

"At first. Then she was fucking livid. Seeing me in the bed, I looked like death. The visions still haunt her and will wake her up in the dead of night. She told me if I was going to die then she didn't want to witness it. She didn't want the last vision she had of me to be a blood-soaked body."

"You need a new job," I grumbled.

She sent me a warning glance. "I won't give it up, Cael."

"I would never ask you to," I promised. "I may hate it, but I'm a Saint. Commitment and dedication to a dangerous occupation are something I can relate to. And, despite what you think, neither will Ethan. You can add me as your contact. Or Ethan if that makes you feel less intimidated."

"You don't intimidate me."

I chuckled. "Sure I do. But we can work with that."

I stretched out beside her, gently sliding my arm underneath so she could lay on my chest. The moment I had her back in my arms, I knew exactly what she had meant: she was my home, my safety, my one place of sanctuary.

"I stink," she warned. "Much worse than almonds."

"After the worst was over, Gabe put a healing salve on you. It's got an anesthetic in it to ease the pain. Is it helping?"

She nodded. "Still stinks, though."

A flicker of emotion floated over me - brief and still too faint to be distinguished, but at least it was something. Whatever he had done was working, and the runes were losing their power.

"My mother was a witch."

"I'd say that's an accurate assumption at this point, yes."

"And I'm perceived as a threat to your kind, your people or whatever. The Saints."

"By some. Not all."

"They marked me to silence me. Or my emotions at least."

"Yes."

"So we are enemies?"

"It's damn unnerving not knowing where this conversation is leading," I grumbled. I let my fingers trail through her hair. "You are not my enemy, Becca."

"But we should be? Sides I don't even understand, waging a war I didn't even know existed a week ago? We are supposed to be enemies?"

I tried to muddle through her comments, fighting to understand where the conversation was leading. When I realized, I let out a long, frustrated sigh. "It's been a long time since I've had to rely on human abilities at conversation so, if I'm wrong, tell me, but what I'm getting here is you trying to find some excuse to run from me."

"Do I look like I'm running anywhere right now?"

"Escaping then. Becca, you ran already, and that didn't work out very well. Do you really want to press your luck again?"

"I endanger you. You endanger me."

"Saints endanger you," I corrected. "Not me."

"You are one and the same. At all times," she whispered. "That's what you told me."

"I was wrong." I slipped my other hand into hers, entwining our fingers over the sheets. "My soul be damned, Becca. It's worthless without you anyway."

"You barely know me."

"I know you better than anyone on the fucking planet. Tell me I'm wrong."

"You're not wrong," she managed. "But-"

"No buts. We're either worth fighting for, or we aren't."

Tears gathered at the edges of her eyes, slowly trickling down onto my chest. She was going to tell me no. I'd made a fool of myself, lost every shred of masculinity with my sappy words and this little demon was going to turn me away and break me into a thousand pieces. As soon as the hurt began to rise, her hand squeezed mine.

"I did fight for you."

That threw me and my words stumbled. "Wait...what?"

"At the cemetery. They asked things about you. Over and over until I couldn't even understand what they wanted. They interrogated me like they did my mother. But it was all about you."

I bristled and nudged her with my shoulder before remembering she couldn't move. "They hurt you because you wouldn't answer questions about me? Are you fucking insane? Becca, I have nothing to hide. I don't need to be protected by anyone much less you. Why didn't you tell us this earlier? Ethan, Gabe?"

"They called you a Judas. They said you would betray the Saints, all of them."

"And you believed them?" I was indignant, but it only lasted for a second. I *was* betraying them by choosing her. She knew that and was doing her damnedest to prevent me from making that choice.

"Becca, I want you to listen to me. Listen to every word I say to you. Anyone who would do this to you, to anyone, does not deserve my loyalty. Or Ethan's or Gabe's. Actually, I can't imagine anyone living at the Row pledging their loyalty to those that would do such a thing. It is not who the Saints are, what we were created for, what we stand for and believe in. This doesn't end here. You have to understand that. We are being betrayed from our very core, and we will solve that whether you are standing beside me or not. If you walk away, you're walking away from me. Nothing more, nothing less, because the only thing that changes is you not being in my arms."

She nodded but remained silent. I didn't need to read her emotions to see the conflict warring inside. When she came to her decision, her voice was a quiet but undeniable promise.

"You are home."

Her guilt was strong enough to power through the runes as if they were invisible and it caused my heart to lurch with relief. I was relieved...she was consumed with guilt. Self-absorbed ass of a Saint that I am, I'd take guilt over my own heartbreak any day.

With a gentle tug, I curled her harder into my chest, wrapping her in the tightest embrace I dared without fear of hurting her. I kissed the top of her head as her tears continued to fall. "Then welcome home, Becca," I murmured, "to Saint's Row."

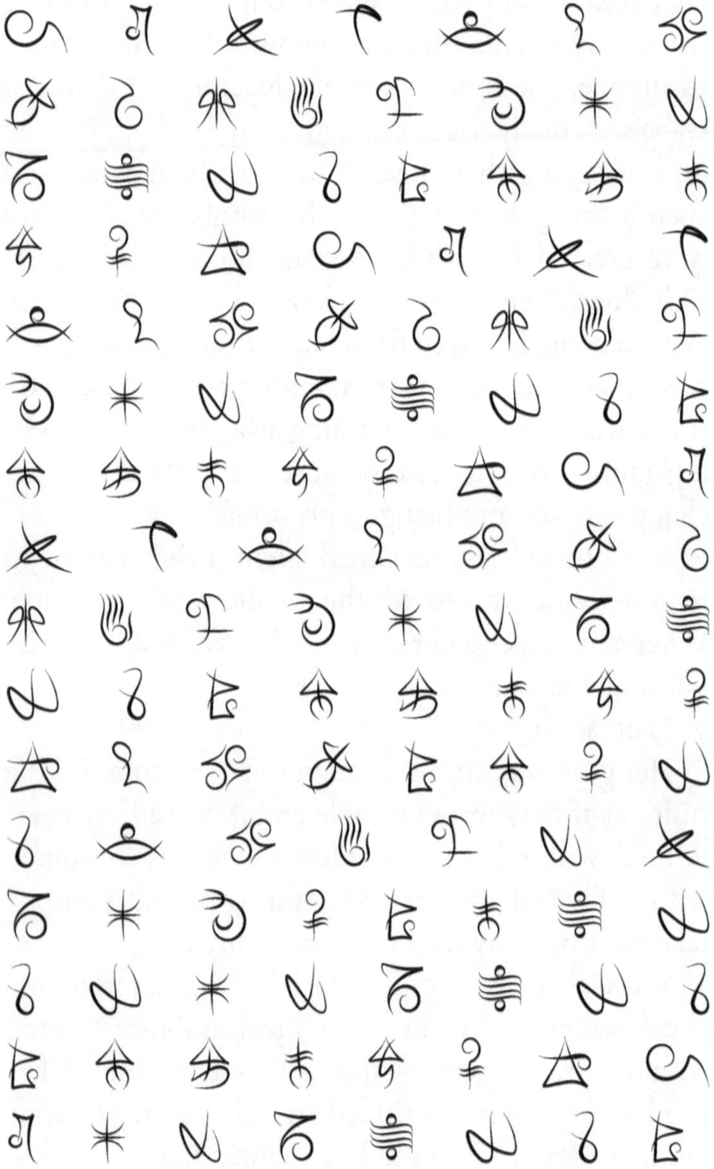

ABOUT THE AUTHOR

Elizabeth Blair writes dark, contemporary fiction with a modern twist to create novels where everyone wants to root for the bad guy. In addition to writing, she works as a rural librarian in Arkansas and holds positions in several state and national library associations. On a rare free weekend, she can be found riding the jeep trails near her home in the national forests or playing World of Warcraft with her family. Visit her online at: www.elizabethblairbooks.com.